HUNTING

SUSPENSE

HUNTING THE CAT

KEITH GRAY

Mammoth

First published in Great Britain 1997
by Mammoth, an imprint of Reed International Books Ltd
Michelin House, 81 Fulham Road, London SW2 6RB
and Auckland, Melbourne, Singapore and Toronto

ISBN 0 7497 2758 6

10 9 8 7 6 5 4 3 2 1

A CIP catalogue record for this title is available from the British Library

Typeset by Avon Dataset Ltd, Bidford on Avon, Warwickshire
Printed in Great Britain by Cox & Wyman Ltd, Reading, Berkshire

Cover photograph from SUPERSTOCK photo library

SUSPENSE

for John

The hills woke reluctantly. The early morning sun had to struggle with a blanket of mist which they seemed anxious to cling to. It lay thick and stagnant across the downs and fells; the grass was stooped, heavy with dew, the spiders' webs could have been spun from brittle glass. It was a veil, a cover under which the hills could keep secret things hidden.

But the sun is ever the optimist. It climbed higher, pushing its thin beams up over the ridges and along the valleys in an effort to pierce the mist's heavy cloak. And from its seat in the sky it may very well have looked as though the hills were clambering on top of each other, vying for the position nearest to its warmth. But from most other, less venerable places, it could be claimed that the hills were burying themselves deeper under one another, wrestling for the dark.

This morning, in one of the places the sun was not yet able to reach, something was wary of the new day. It stood over the kill; the bloody sheep's chine was bitten and ripped, the grass spattered like the dirty wool, a string of ligament across the rock. It listened to the sounds of the chill dawn. It smelt the approach of the morning. It could feel the hills' unwillingness to give up the secrecy of the night, and knew that it could very well be the reason why.

But its hunger was once more abated. It moved quickly, quietly through the long grass. It knew dark places the sun could never even dream of.

Chapter One

The windscreen-wipers hissed and returned, hissed and returned. 'Becksall 12' read the sign as it shot by at the side of the road. The puddles sprayed high around the Land-Rover's wheels.

'Not far now.'

The fields unfolded around them, one after the other behind the hedges and trees running along either side of the winding country road. A car, a big Vauxhall, sped by in the opposite direction. There was a whooshing sound and the Land-Rover rocked gently on its suspension.

The father and son sat in silence, both watching the road ahead. Don, the father, was feeling anxious. The silence was heavy on him. He glanced up at the grey sky, frustrated, and cursed the weather. The rain would spoil the weekend. But the forecast had said it would be dry; chilly maybe, but still dry. He'd had this trip planned for weeks. It was important to him in so many different ways.

'There's today's paper somewhere in the back,' he said, jabbing a thumb over his shoulder. 'If you're bored.' He looked out of the corner of his eye at his son sitting in the passenger seat. 'It's only a shower,' he said, 'it won't last long.'

Joseph didn't answer. The sky was dull and low for as far as he could see. The clouds had closed in around midday, and his mood had closed in with them.

His father reached across and switched the stereo on. A dance tune stuttered and crackled out of the speakers hidden in the Land-Rover's doors. 'Have you got a tape with you?' he asked. 'The reception's terrible out here. Not that they play anything worth listening to on Radio One any more, eh?' He grinned at his son. Then when Joseph didn't answer, Don said, 'Come on, your mum told me you'd packed your Walkman. You must have brought a tape with you.'

The boy sighed, unbuckled his seat belt and crawled over the seat into the back.

'And bring that paper with you,' his father called over his shoulder.

Joseph hunted through his rucksack; he'd forgotten exactly where he'd put his Walkman. But he found a tape in one of the side pockets with the camera he'd been given for his birthday, and clambered back into the front with it. He'd left the paper on the back seat.

'Put it on,' his father said. 'Who is it? East 17?'

Joseph shook his head scornfully. 'No.'

'I thought they were meant to be popular these days.'

'Only if you're nine.' Joseph pushed the tape into the machine.

'Oh, I see. So who's this then? Anybody I know?'

'Alanis Morissette,' Joseph told him.

His father shook his head. 'No, never heard of him.'

'It's a her.'

'Oh, sorry.' His father chuckled quietly. 'Never heard of her either.'

Joseph was fifteen today. Which wasn't old enough. He wanted to be sixteen; he wanted to be old enough to leave home.

They drove on in silence – except for Alanis. Don pretended to like the music. Theirs was the only vehicle on the road; the fields were flat, and high up in the cockpit of the Land-Rover it was easy to see the empty road unwinding before them over the top of the hedgerows. The hills were getting closer, but were

5

still hazy behind the gauze-like sheet of rain. A bedraggled and sagging scarecrow didn't look up from his field as they sped by.

Joseph watched his father as he drove. He tapped his fingers on the steering wheel, not quite in time with the music. He was a tall, slim man with very dark hair and heavy eyebrows. He had what Joseph always thought of as a 'Flintstone Face'; the blue shadow of a beard which needs shaving at least twice a day. But his dark hair was beginning to recede slightly now. Instead of being parted and brushed back on top of his head, it had been cut short and combed forward, giving him the perfect widow's peak. Joseph wondered if his father's hair was the only thing which had changed about him in the past five years. He searched his face for anything which didn't quite match up with the old memories. He could see the signs of ageing, showing through as if his youth were peeling away like flaky paint to reveal the old man beneath. He still had that dimple in his chin however, like the one John Travolta has. He'd always told Joseph it was a chin-button, like a belly-button, only better. And when he'd been younger Joseph had wanted one so badly that he'd even gone as far as trying to make one with a knitting-needle.

But whenever anybody told him he reminded them of his father nowadays, there was a hot resentment burning deep inside his belly which he found hard to disguise.

'Becksall 9'. The rain seemed to be letting up slightly, even though the thick, grey clouds still limped their way across the sky. Don switched the wipers to intermittent.

'There's a nice pub just beyond the village where we can stop for something to eat if you like.'

Joseph shrugged.

'It could be the last decent meal we get,' Don said, 'unless you can catch us something big.' He grinned across at his son who didn't answer, but continued to stare out at the road ahead. Don fidgeted in his seat. He leaned forward to stretch his shoulders, shuffled his backside around a bit. But it wasn't the seat that was making him uncomfortable.

Joseph had been ten years old. It had been a Tuesday. He'd come home from school expecting lasagne and chips for his tea; expecting to get into trouble because of the mud and grass stains on the knees of his trousers from playing football, and expecting to have to lie about completing his home-work so he could get down to the park to finish the game before it got dark. Instead his mother had told him that his father had left home.

They came to a crossroads. The sign for Becksall pointed down the road away to the left, and Don followed its direction. Joseph watched the way the low cloud scraped the tops of the hills.

He'd been eleven years old and he'd no longer been able to see his mother and father in the same room as each other. He'd no longer been able to sit up late watching videos with his father while his mother complained that he'd be tired for school in the morning. He'd no longer been able to help his father choose the numbers for his Pools coupon. And he'd no longer been able to stand and watch his father shave, talking about how they'd spend the millions when they won . . . He'd no longer been able to go to sleep at night without wondering what his father was doing.

He'd been twelve and he'd had to put on a new shirt and tie to meet Trudy, his father's new girlfriend. She wore suits, carried a Vodafone and called him Jason. He'd been thirteen and had brought Johnny back from playing football for a drink at his house, when he'd seen his mother and Roger, the ginger-haired junior school teacher, kissing in the kitchen. He'd also been thirteen when he was put on report at school for fighting with Johnny in the dining-hall.

'At least all this rain will keep the fish happy,' Don tried. 'Maybe we should have a bet. What do you say? Whoever lands the biggest catch of the weekend gets lunch bought for them on the way home on Tuesday. Sound good to you?'

Joseph shrugged. 'If you want.'

'Just as long as your pockets are deep enough to buy me a proper meal. I don't want fobbing off with a tatty old McDonald's.' Don was smiling again.

Joseph wasn't. He'd been fourteen, three weeks from his fifteenth birthday, exactly twenty-one days ago, and his mother had told him that his father was coming back to live with them. But by then it was already much too late.

'Becksall 5'. They could see the village now, the houses looking tiny against the backdrop of the hills. The hills which suddenly made Joseph think of the villain in a pantomime; They're behind you! he wanted to shout. The road seemed to be getting narrower as it snaked its way through the countryside.

His father had appeared unexpectedly in July. He'd appeared in his new Land-Rover with a new job, and he'd taken Joseph and his mother for a drive in his new Land-Rover to show them where he worked at his new job. It was with an estate agent's or a solicitor's or somewhere, (somewhere with three names on the sign above its offices anyway) and his father had been all excited; childlike in his sheer enthusiasm for the sudden leap forward he claimed his career had taken. Not that Joseph could understand why; it wasn't as if his father's name was one of the three on the sign above the offices.

Maybe he should have listened more to what his father was saying, maybe then he would have understood, but what Joseph couldn't get out of his mind was the fact that this was the first time he'd seen his parents talk to each other in virtually five years. His father had always been around, he'd never left town, but he'd never come to the house unless it was to pick Joseph up for his allotted time, and then he'd always waited in the car. But it seemed as though his excitement about the new job had broken down any barriers for him; he was suddenly talking about new futures, fresh hope. And seeing them together had somehow offended Joseph. Five years had been such a long time for him. How dare his father talk to his mother after all that time? She had nothing to do with him any more. She was Joseph's, not his. His father was suddenly an intruder. The man was long since unwelcome anyway, so how dare he trespass now?

Don had said he would take Joseph out for a meal that evening, and Joseph had dutifully changed into his best pair of trousers, the pair his grandma had bought for him, thinking it was expected. But his mother had come upstairs and told him to wear the ones his father had given him for Christmas. And then his mother had put on her new dress and all three of them had driven to The Baton Rouge in town. To celebrate. Apparently.

Then the following week the three of them had spent the day at Alton Towers. Joseph had been left to wander the amusements on his own with his pockets full of his father's change, while his parents strolled through the gardens on the beautiful sunny day. He'd taken a ride in the cable car and dropped the coins out of the window one by one. There was an evening at the bowling alley. There was a trip to the cinema. Then there was another meal at another posh restaurant, but this time it was Joseph who wasn't invited.

He'd sat at home on his own. He'd played his music as loudly as the little tape deck in his bedroom would allow him. He'd remembered being ten years old and being woken up in the middle of the night by his mother's crying. He'd remembered lying awake in bed knowing that he'd have to go through into her bedroom and comfort her, hold her, tell her how much he still loved her. But he'd also remembered wishing that just for once she'd come into his and do it for him. He'd only been ten and he'd had to carry the weight of her sadness and loneliness and guilt as well as his own. He'd tried to understand how his mother could have forgotten so easily, because he didn't think he ever could.

The road twisted and turned, the sharp bends forcing the Land-Rover to slow down. But it only ever led them closer to the hills. 'Becksall 2'. They looked like a tidal wave, Joseph decided. They reared up behind the village ready to crash down on the small houses.

'They look magnificent, don't they?' Don said. 'Incredible.' His eyes flicked between the road and the hills. Then to Joseph. It was obvious he wanted his son to share in what he was feeling. It was like lending a record to a friend and trying to get them to hear it and appreciate it exactly the way you did. 'They're just like I remember them. Simply breathtaking.' He smiled at his son. 'And at least it's stopped raining. It looks like the sun might make an appearance after all.' He even tried to hum the chorus of the song coming out of the stereo.

Joseph didn't think the sun would make the slightest bit of difference.

They were going to freeze. Camping in September was a stupid idea. Camping in the rain in those hills in September was an utterly ridiculous idea. He'd only agreed to come to keep his mother happy. He didn't want to be here. He didn't enjoy camping. And he didn't like his father.

He wasn't stupid. He knew what this birthday treat, this surprise weekend fishing trip, was all in aid of. He was the fly in the ointment, a problem, it didn't take a genius to work it out. His parents wanted things back to how they used to be, back to the 'good old days' and 'happy families' times, but he was stopping that from happening. So here he was, alone with his father for three nights, away from everybody else in the whole world on this 'getting to know you' session for the Walker men, this experiment in male bonding for the estranged father and son. It was laughable really. His father must have watched too many Disney movies.

The sign read, 'Becksall Welcomes Careful Drivers' and houses sprang up on either side of the road. Old, grey houses looking as though they were leaning against each other for support. Very few had the neatly-met red bricks of modern buildings, and several could have almost entirely been made from ivy. There was the stone cross of a war memorial, a tiny Post Office and an overgrown orchard half-buried by windfalls, then the village was behind them. Only the hills lay in front.

'What did you do with the paper?' Don asked.

'It's still in the back.'

'Would you fetch it for me, please?'

Joseph didn't move.

'Come on, Joe. There's something I want to show you.' He was trying so hard to be light-hearted.

'Don't be such a sourpuss, it's your birthday.'

Reluctantly Joseph climbed into the back to get the paper. But he sat on the back seat with it, not willing to give in completely to his father's wishes.

Don watched him in the rear-view mirror. 'I just thought that today of all days would be the best time for you to read your stars,' he said. 'They should be as close as they're ever going to be on your birthday.'

'I never read my stars.'

'Nor do I. Unless it's my birthday.'

Joseph was about to climb back into the front.

'Come on. It's only meant to be a bit of fun. Read them out. See what they've got to say.' Don winked at his son through the mirror's reflection. 'They might tell you just how cold you're going to get in that tent of ours tonight.'

Joseph sighed and shuffled through the paper's pages.

'I think they're near the back,' Don told him.

He found them and scanned the columns looking for Virgo, 22nd August to 22nd September. Then he read aloud. 'You are right to feel apprehensive at the beginning of your new year. Last-minute changes to your plans may be needed. Be willing to back down on certain issues, but never admit defeat. Whatever it is looming on your horizon, try not to dismiss it. It won't go away on its own.'

'Is that it?'

Joseph nodded.

'Oh well,' Don said. 'As vague as ever, I suppose.'

The hills seemed to open up to let them in along the narrow road. They rose high on either side, crowding out the sun which had only just managed to break free of the clouds. And if either Joseph or his father had bothered to check over their shoulder or glance in the rear-view mirror, they would have seen the road quickly disappear behind them as if the hills had closed in again to swallow it up.

Chapter Two

But if the hills had looked like a tidal wave behind the village, then they must surely look as though they'd already swamped The Retreat.

The little pub was on the peak of a green wave, being washed far out into the green rolling sea all around. Don had gone on and on about how beautiful the hills looked, but Joseph didn't think he could have thought of a much more ill-suited description for the countryside. The word 'beautiful' had always made him think of something that sparkled, or shone, or something that smiled. And the hills did none of these things.

Don pulled the Land-Rover off the road and into the lay-by which served as a carpark for the pub. He switched the engine off. 'Right,' he said, 'let's get us something to eat.'

'I'm not hungry.'

'But we haven't had anything since we set out

this morning. I think you should at least have something.'

'No, thanks. I'm really not hungry.'

Don sighed. He unbuckled his seat belt. 'Well I am. And it might be a good idea to get some directions, just in case my memory's not up to scratch.'

'I'll wait here for you.'

'Come on. I'll buy you a drink.'

'I'm fine.'

Don had his hand on the door handle, but he hesitated. 'You're not going to make this very easy for me, are you?' he said.

Joseph frowned. 'What d'you mean?'

But his father shook his head. 'Nothing.' He smiled again, if a little awkwardly. 'Listen, I'm starved, and I'm not about to leave you sitting out here on your own. Put your coat on and let's go see what The Retreat has to offer me for my tea, OK?'

Joseph's frown deepened but Don pretended not to notice. Joseph climbed out of the Land-Rover reluctantly and made sure he stayed two or three paces behind his father all the way up to the little pub's front door. He knew he was being difficult. But that was the way he wanted to be. He pushed himself further down into his mood. It was a wall, a barrier he could keep between them. He may not have been able to express the way he felt in words, but he knew he wanted to keep the man at arm's length.

The Retreat was very warm and quite dark inside. The floor was made of stone slabs and was uneven. The bar was on the left as they walked in, several hand pumps in a row, only one electric pump for lager. On the right was a wooden partition sectioning off a small area of the pub; it had a stained glass window of red and green diamonds set into it. A real fire crackled behind a cluster of small round tables at the far wall. The lights on the walls looked like old-fashioned oil lamps, but were easy to spot as imitations with their slender light bulbs instead of wicks. There was a large black-and-white aerial-view photograph of what looked like Becksall above the bar; the tiny village nestled amongst a ragged pattern of fields, the hills casting their shadow. A large portrait of a man and his dog hung above the fire. The man carried a shotgun broken open over his arm whilst the dog had a bird, a pheasant, lolling in its mouth. Don and Joseph seemed to be the only customers.

Don approached the bar just as a woman appeared

behind it from out of a back room. She had to walk sideways like a crab, because otherwise she'd be too wide to fit in the small gap between bar and counter. She was drying her hands on a dish-cloth. She didn't smile. 'We don't serve minors,' she said, looking at Joseph. Her frizzy, ginger hair glowed like an angry aura in the dim light. Her balloon of a blue-flowered smock was tied in a bow at the neck. It was short-sleeved and the pasty flesh of her upper arms rippled as she vigorously rubbed her hands and wrists with the dish-cloth. She stood her ground behind the long, wooden handles of the hand pumps.

'We were just after something to eat, actually,' Don said.

'Lunch is up till two,' the landlady told him. 'It's nearly three now.'

'We'd be happy with a sandwich . . .'

'Lunch is up till two,' she repeated.

'I see.' Don shrugged his shoulders at Joseph, then turned back to the fat landlady. 'I don't suppose there's anywhere else close by where we could get something, is there? Back in the village maybe?'

And suddenly a voice behind Joseph piped up. 'Go on, Lizzie. Making a sandwich won't kill you.'

Both Joseph and his father turned around to see an old man sitting at a table behind them. He'd been hidden by the partition when they'd first walked in.

'The bairn looks half-starved. Make him one of your specials, Lizzie.'

But the woman wasn't all that willing to back down. 'There's laws,' she told the old man. 'We don't serve minors.'

'He don't want serving. He wants a sandwich.' The landlady scowled at him. Not that he seemed to notice. He took a mouthful of his beer, swallowed hard, and said to Joseph with a wink, 'Best sandwich-maker for miles around is our Lizzie.' Then he turned back to the woman. 'What harm's he gonna be as skinny as that? Mebbe with a couple of your sandwiches inside of him he'd be worth throwing out.'

Unbelievably, the woman's scowl darkened even more.

Don looked uncomfortable. 'That's all right,' he said, 'we really don't want to be any trouble.' He took a step towards the door.

'Ham or cheese,' Lizzie said. It was far from a question.

Don hesitated. 'Er, well. If you're sure it's no . . .'

'Ham or cheese. We've run out of corned beef.'

'Right,' Don said. 'Right, thank you. Ham will be fine for me. What about you, Joseph?'

The boy shrugged. He hadn't liked the way he'd been used in the argument. Not that it was anything new to him of course; his parents had often used him in their arguments. 'I'm not hungry,' he said.

Lizzie tutted. Don looked anxious.

The old man said, 'He'll have ham too, Lizzie.' He completely ignored Joseph. 'It'll do him wonders, one of your ham sandwiches.' He drained the last of his pint and held his empty glass aloft. 'And I'll have another Old Peculier, if you would, my love.'

Don thanked Lizzie uncertainly, then led Joseph over to introduce themselves to the old man while the woman disappeared, crab-like, into the back room again. They each pulled up a stool to the table and the man stood up to shake hands with them in turn. Joseph took his hand tentatively, a little nervous of his brashness. He was unsure whether he should feel indignant or not. He would have stood his ground against his father.

He looked the old man over. He guessed at about

sixty. The sleeves of his white shirt were rolled up and the collar was open, his dark trousers were pressed with sharp creases. He was a big man, but what must have been muscle when he'd been younger looked to be going soft now. He had a flabby face, a double chin, but he was cleanly shaven. His eyebrows were white above his large, watery eyes, but his hair was thick and jet-black. It looked a little too small for his head. And Joseph was quick to realise it was a wig. The old man gave the impression of someone who didn't really know how to dress up smart, but was trying all the same.

'Didn't she send my beer over?' he tutted.

'Do you want me to call her back?' Don asked.

But the old man shook his head. 'Better not,' he said, 'she can be a right moody beggar when she wants.' He leaned in closer to the two of them as if to confide some great secret. 'Knew her father years ago; he was a nasty piece of work too, never did like him. You know I've been coming here for nigh on forty years and they still won't let me bring my dog in. I don't suppose you saw an old collie outside when you came, did you?' Both Don and Joseph shook their heads. And the old man nodded to show that it was what he'd expected. 'Aye. The lad probably got bored and went home. He does that.'

'I hope we didn't cause any ill feeling back then,' Don said.

'Don't matter if you did. She thrives on ill feeling, that one. I told you: it's in her blood.'

'Is it just her who runs the place?'

'No, there's her husband, Alan.' The old man shrugged. 'He's not a bad sort, just married the wrong woman. He's just as fat, though. Little wonder they haven't got kids when you see the size of them together. They can't fit behind the bar at the same time so I doubt they've got much chance in a bed.'

Don was quite taken aback by this. He glanced in an embarrassed kind of way at Joseph. And with that, fat Lizzie appeared again, carrying a plate with their ham sandwiches on. Joseph couldn't help but watch her in a different way as she lumbered across the stone floor towards them. The white plate was cracked and the sandwiches (both of them) looked flat and limp. They certainly didn't look 'special' in any way, and Joseph guessed the old man had known that all along.

'Two pound,' she said.

Don offered her a smile along with the coins. 'Thank you.'

'There's no more ham.'

'These will be fine, thank you.'

She muttered to herself and waddled away again. But before she reached the bar the old man called after her, 'And that pint of Peculier when you're ready please, Lizzie. In fact, make that two. Mr Walker here looks like he's thirsty. And I reckon the bairn'll have . . .'

'I don't serve minors.'

'Serve me then,' he said. 'I've been wanting a cool glass of pop all day.' He smiled at fat Lizzie's scowl. 'She only keeps her custom 'cos she's the only pub this side of the village,' he told Don.

Joseph looked at the sandwiches. They both had chubby palm prints on them where she'd pressed the top round of bread flat. He pushed the plate away from him. 'I don't want this,' he said.

'Come on,' Don said, 'it'll fill a gap.' He picked up his sandwich and took a bite.

Joseph shook his head. 'I told you, I'm not hungry.'

Don looked slightly awkward with the other man

listening in. 'I'd eat it if I were you. It'll be suppertime before we get anything else.'

Joseph felt the tiny thrill of having the upper hand over his father in front of the stranger. 'You have it then. I don't want it.' He dared his father to challenge him further.

And Don did make a move to say something else, but before he could open his mouth the old man tutted loudly and said, 'Don't be such a pain in the backside and do as you're told, sonny.'

Joseph was shocked. The comment was like a slap across the face. He'd never been spoken to like that before. He went to defend himself but didn't know quite what to say.

Don gave a kind of embarrassed-sounding cough. 'Yes . . . well . . .' he started, but didn't finish.

And that was how they met Tom Beverly.

Chapter Three

The sandwich tasted as bad as it looked. Joseph picked at it reluctantly. The bread was dry and the ham was slimy. Even his glass of Coke was warm and flat and tasted more like Kwik Save Cola than the real thing. He wondered if his father's drink tasted any better. 'Old Peculier' Tom had called it, and it looked like a pint of purple tar with a dirty-white head. Don had refused the drink at first because he was driving, but had quickly owned up to being less than an angel and seemed to be enjoying it now.

'I've lived in the hills ever since I left the army,' Tom was saying, in answer to Don's question. 'My grandfather was a sheep-farmer and I reckoned that it was just about the perfect job for me too. And as it turned out, it pretty much was at that. I found I had a talent and good love for it in the end.'

'So why did you retire?' Don asked.

'The wife. She'd been pushing me for years to pack it in. She kept on telling me she was fed up to the back teeth of having me looking scruffy all the time, trailing mud and sheep muck through her house. She said that it was undignified at our age; said it was time we settled down to think about each other instead of the sheep.'

Don laughed. 'So she finally talked you into it, did she?'

'She died,' Tom said. '17th July. And I sold the sheep for slaughter the very next day.'

Don's grin slipped. 'Oh . . . Oh, I'm so sorry.'

Tom drained the last of his pint. 'Not your fault,' he said. Then, 'Care for another?'

Don shook his head and held up his glass to show that he still had almost half a pint left in it. 'No, I really should go steady. Makes me wish I wasn't driving, though.'

'Yeah, it's good stuff. Puts hairs on your chest, as my father used to say.' Tom got to his feet with a small grunt of forced breath. 'Don't mind if I have another, do you?'

Don shook his head. 'No, not at all. But this one's on me, OK?'

Tom sat back down again without hesitation. 'Good of you,' he said. And Don stood up to go to the bar.

Joseph felt a little uncomfortable sitting alone with the old man while his father tried to coax fat Lizzie out from the back room. He wasn't used to anyone being quite so forward, and couldn't work out whether it made the old man rude or just plain honest. He got the impression that Tom didn't like him very much. He made Joseph feel like a whiny little kid, and that Tom had much better things to do than sit and listen to one of them. But Joseph knew he wasn't like that, not really; he knew there was good reason for the bitterness he felt towards his father. He found himself wanting to be liked by the old man, and wanting to explain why he was acting like he was. In fact he had the words on the tip of his tongue . . . but then his father returned with the drinks.

'I got myself another anyway,' Don said, sitting himself down. 'I don't think Lizzie would have been too happy with me if I'd dragged her out of the back just for the one.'

Tom laughed. 'Aye, you're probably right.'

'Does this place ever get busy?' Don asked, taking a sip of purple tar and looking around himself at the empty tables.

Tom nodded. 'Give them time to knock off and

they'll all be here,' he said. He made a good start on his fresh pint. 'So what brings you to Becksall?' he asked.

'We're on a fishing trip.' Don beamed at Joseph as he said this. 'It's Joe's birthday and we thought we'd get away for the weekend, just the two of us.'

'You'll be heading for The Leap, then? That's the best fishing there is around here.'

Don nodded. 'Yes. That's the place. Am I right in thinking there's a road that takes us all of the way up to the river?'

But Tom shook his head. 'Not any more there isn't. You're going back a few years if you can still remember that.'

Joseph listened to the two men talk. Don told the older man all about his new job, which he was still very excited about, but which must have been on the verge of boring Tom to tears. At least that was how Joseph felt, anyway. The conversation veered from one to the other, something one man said reminding the second that he had thoughts on that particular subject too, or that he'd also experienced something similar, or a friend of his had anyway, then back again.

Don seemed to find what the older man had to say riveting; all the talk about living in the hills, right next door to nature and the like. Joseph knew it had always been his father's ambition to retire to the middle of the countryside somewhere, and wondered if Becksall was quickly becoming an option for him. But the boy let most of what was said wash over him. He only half-listened because he was only half-invited to join in. It was like most of the conversations he'd experienced with adults; they'd always much rather talk to each other than to any kids that just happened to be present. He was asked questions when they remembered he was still there, but that was about all. He was never asked an opinion. Which was a pity really, as he had several.

It started to get dark outside and, as Tom had promised, the small pub gradually began to fill up. But only with men; none of them seemed to have brought their wives or girlfriends along for the evening. They all knew Tom, nodding their greetings or offering a hello, and Tom gave his informed opinion on each of them: a tall man was lazy but had a pretty wife; a bald man with glasses wasn't the sort of bloke you'd want on your side in a fight, while a youngish man with straggly blond hair was quickly and nastily denounced as a worthless, greasy-faced lout.

Joseph sat and watched a few of the men play darts while his father and Tom talked (the dartboard was the reason for the wood and stained glass partition separating this part of the pub from the rest). His father was soon drinking his third pint of Old Peculier while Tom was easily on his fifth, and that wasn't counting the one he'd had when they'd first arrived nearly two hours before. Joseph wondered if his father had forgotten about having to drive the Land-Rover, but decided he wasn't going to be the one to remind him.

It was obvious the drink was getting to Don; he accidentally knocked over an empty pint glass, twice, and his voice became a little too loud. Joseph had only ever seen his father drunk once before, at a Christmas party before his parents had separated. He could only vaguely remember what had happened, none of the details, only really that it had ended in a huge argument between his mum and dad.

Tom was getting drunk as well, but in a very different way. The older man seemed to be getting more and more oppressive with each successive drink.

He was becoming more critical of the other men in the pub, his words becoming spiteful, even aggressive towards them. The drink seemed to be fuelling a certain, pointed hostility within him. Their conversation slipped from small talk about wives and work to politics and religion. And Joseph was completely forgotten now. So he got up to go to the toilet.

He guessed he'd probably get into trouble for wandering off in a pub full of strangers and not telling his father where he was going . . . But then again, would he? Would his father dare to tell him off? He reckoned he held a certain power over his parents at the moment. He knew they were trying everything they could to please him, to make him happy, to have things exactly as they used to be before his father had left. He liked that power. It gave him some armour against his father trying to mess up his life. When he'd first been told about this fishing trip by his mother he'd immediately known what it was all in aid of, but he'd also realised that he was in some way actually in control of how it could all turn out.

The door to the gents was by the side of the bar. Fat Lizzie scowled her frizzy, red scowl at him, but he wasn't sure whether it was because she didn't relieve minors or because she was rushed off her feet with all the other customers. And her husband hadn't appeared to offer any help, either. But Joseph ignored her anyway.

The toilet was cramped and smelly. Each of the three urinals had their own personal puddle, and someone with horrible, scrawly handwriting had put an 'out of order' sign on the hand dryer. The man with straggly blond hair (the worthless, greasy-faced lout) was in there when Joseph went in, holding himself in one hand and his pint in the other. He was standing at the centre urinal forcing Joseph to squeeze in between him and the wall. He could only have been in his early twenties; his face was pockmarked as if he'd suffered from bad acne as a teenager, and his collar-length hair was in desperate need of a comb. Joseph tried to ignore him, but the young man seemed to want a conversation.

'You Tom Beverly's grandson, then?' he asked, his words more than a little slurred, obviously drunk.

Joseph shook his head and tried to pee as quickly as he possibly could. He felt trapped and vulnerable.

'That's good,' the young man said. Then added nastily, 'I'd hate to be that old git's grandson.'

Joseph didn't look at him; he kept his head down. He just wanted to get out of the toilet and back into the busy pub again as quickly as possible.

But the young man leaned in towards him, forcing him closer up against the cold wall. 'His wife was mad, you know.' He nodded to confirm his own words. 'Yeah. Used to see things.'

Joseph had no idea what he was talking about, and was beginning to doubt whether the young man himself did either. He was unsteady on his feet, his knees sagging as if the weight of his body was a little too much for them to handle.

'I reckon he drove her to it, myself. That's what my dad says too. Lovely woman she was. Always friendly, always ready to listen to your problems. What she was doing with him out there I'll never know.'

Joseph finished, but because the young man was leaning in so close to him he couldn't move away. He would have to physically push past him to get out of the little corner in which he was trapped. And for some reason, he really didn't want to have to touch this greasy-faced lout.

'He didn't use to be so bad. Never friendly like she was, but, you know, always . . .' He searched for a word. 'Always . . .' He swayed a little and seemed to forget he hadn't finished his sentence. 'All he does is sit in here all day now, thinking he's better than the rest of us. Sold his sheep and spends all his money on drink.'

The young man finished, and while he tried to simultaneously zip himself back up and take a swig from his glass, Joseph saw a gap and ducked into it. But the young man stepped backwards, blocking his way. And Joseph wasn't sure if he'd done it on purpose, or if his knees had finally given way and he'd had to steady himself from falling over. Whichever, he also lost his grip on the glass and it dropped from his fingers to shatter across the stone floor. The noise was much too loud as it bounced off the close walls. Joseph's trainers were spattered with beer.

'Awww!' the young man wailed. 'Awww, hell!' He turned bleary eyes on Joseph. 'Sorry, mate,' he said.

Joseph shook his head. 'That's OK. Don't worry about it.' He was edging his way towards the door.

'Good of you to say so. I wouldn't *mean* to waste good beer, would I?'

Again Joseph shook his head.

'It's not like I'd do it on purpose, is it? I'm not like that.'

Joseph had his hand on the door handle. But the young man grabbed his shoulder. 'Let me buy you a drink. I like you.'

'That's OK.' Joseph shook the hand off, pushed down the handle and swung the door open to step back into the pub's smoky main room. 'Thanks anyway.' And he quickly headed through the group of men standing around the bar, back to the table where his father and Tom Beverly were sitting. He turned around just in time to see the young man come out of the toilet looking for him, and he sat down as low as he possibly could on his stool, hunching himself up.

His father didn't even seem to have noticed that he'd gone anywhere, but Tom saw him checking over his shoulder nervously. The old man squinted through the smoke and dim light, following the boy's anxious glances. His face darkened when he spotted the greasy-faced lout making his way over to their table. 'He giving you trouble?' Tom asked.

Joseph wasn't sure what to say. 'Not really,' was the best he could come up with.

Tom stood up as the young man approached them. 'What can we do for you, Trevor?' There was suspicion in the old man's eyes.

Trevor shrugged. 'I just wanted to offer my friend a drink, that's all. Nothing wrong with that, is there?' Behind the beer-induced glaze, there was malice in the young man's gaze.

'I can't remember the boy telling me you were a friend of his.'

'Just now. We just made friends. Just this minute.' He swayed slightly on those weak knees of his, leaning over Joseph with a hand planted firmly on the boy's shoulder. 'Didn't we, eh?' He grinned mockingly up at Tom. 'Had a good chat, didn't we?'

For the second time that afternoon, Joseph found himself to be the centre of somebody else's argument. But this time it felt quite different. There was an almost physical tension in the air. He realised that most of the other men in the room were watching them. And that this was very probably the continuation of an old feud.

'He's not having a drink, Trevor,' Tom said. 'Leave the boy alone.'

'How'd you know? He might want one.'

'Not from you, he doesn't. And not in here.'

'He can have one if he likes. I'm buying it for him.' The grip on Joseph's shoulder was getting harder and slightly painful as the young man used it to hold himself upright. 'What d'you want, matey? Take no notice of Grandad here. Anything you like.' Stale beer breath leaked through the grin he aimed at Joseph.

But the boy didn't have time to answer, because Tom suddenly shouted, 'Lizzie! Hey, Lizzie!'

'Can't you see I'm busy?' the irate landlady shouted back. 'Come and queue like the rest of them.'

'The boy, Lizzie,' Tom called to her. 'I was wondering . . .'

'I don't serve minors!' she shrieked.

And Tom turned to the young man with an acid smile on his face. 'House rules, Trevor. Nothing to do with me,' he said.

Trevor didn't say a word, not even to Joseph. He simply turned his back and started to walk away.

Don, who was struck dumb up until this point, said, 'Well, what on earth was that all about?'

But the greasy-faced lout muttered something under his breath as he pushed past a couple of the darts players, and although Joseph didn't quite catch the comment, Tom leaped to his feet, banging into the table hard enough to spill the drinks. He grabbed Trevor by the collar, virtually hauling him off his feet. 'What was that?' the old man bellowed. 'What did you say?' He yanked on the collar in his bunched-up fist. Trevor jerked backwards and almost fell over. Probably would have done if Tom's grip hadn't been quite so strong.

'Get off. Get off me.' Trevor squirmed in vain. 'I never said a word.'

The whole of The Retreat fell silent. Tom's face was red, bloated; he had rage in his eyes now. The younger man was either feeble or had drunk his strength away; it was almost comical, the way he struggled. He was the only one who moved, wriggling on the end of Tom Beverly's arm. Everyone else was a statue, no one spoke.

Then, quietly enough to let the menace in his voice be felt, Tom said, 'You say one more word about my wife, you dare to even mention her name, and I'll kill you. You hear me, boy? I'll kill you.' He let go and Trevor floundered and then fell. No one bothered to pick him up. He had to get to his own feet, unsteady as they were, and walk away. He headed for the bar.

Joseph knew someone like Trevor at school, a boy called Phil Morley. He was always in trouble, always *causing* trouble. Phil didn't know when enough was enough; he simply didn't understand how far he could push things. Either that or he just wasn't able to give in. He'd been in trouble with teachers and the police *so* many times. Too many times. Forever making things worse for himself by insisting on having the final word.

Trevor reminded Joseph very much of this boy when he said, 'She was a lunatic, anyway.'

And Tom Beverly exploded across the room.

Chapter Four

Fat Lizzie howled. The Retreat erupted as *en masse*, the men surged forwards to try and stop Tom Beverly from getting his hands on the worthless, greasy-faced lout. It was an instant explosion of violence in the quiet pub, and all Joseph could do was stare. Tables went flying, glass shattered across the stone floor. The scrum of men shouted and swore at each other, shoving and pushing, heads thrown back, hands raised. Some were protecting Trevor, others holding Tom back. And Tom shouted louder than any of them. He was fighting against them. Joseph had seen fights before, he'd been involved in several on the playground, but nothing so sudden, so chaotic and confused. A trigger had been pulled and there was pandemonium in the little country pub. The wood and stained glass partition shuddered violently as somebody banged into it.

Don stood up. He thought he should be doing something. He was the only man not involved, not shouting and swearing and threatening. He took a single, tentative step. Then stood there awkwardly, not knowing what the hell he would do, even if he did make a move. So he put a hand on his son's shoulder. 'Stay back,' he said, 'don't go getting yourself involved.'

One man fell over as the bodies heaved, and popped out of the mass to sprawl on the cold floor. Another tried to help him up but he too was knocked flat. They were soon on their feet. But they all seemed to be fighting one another to stop Tom and Trevor. It was a mad crush to get to the two in the centre.

Fat Lizzie's husband and partner in fridge-crime appeared from out of the back room. He was bigger than his wife, tall as well as obese, but his voice couldn't be heard over everybody else's. Shouting was getting him nowhere. He waded into the middle of the scrum, belly first.

Unbelievably, Tom had managed to fend off the men trying to restrain him and had somehow got a grip on Trevor's shirt. But someone else had hold of his other fist and all he could do was yank viciously at the young man's clothes.

Trevor was only making things worse for himself.

He prodded and pointed his finger at Tom, goading him on, inciting him into an even higher rage. 'Come on then, Grandad! Come on then!' His face was scrunched up and snarling as he shouted obscenities at the old man. In the middle of the turmoil he knew he was safe – as long as he had the rest of the pub between him and Tom.

But now the landlord had the young man's collar in his massive fist. He jerked him right off his feet, not exactly plucking him out from the crowd, more like dragging him through it. The shirt ripped and Trevor slipped to the floor. But Alan simply picked him up by the scruff of the neck, ignoring his yelps.

Tom was still shouting and struggling, but most of the others (except the ones holding the old man back) were quiet now that Alan had things in hand. They retreated a few steps, giving room, watching for the inevitable outcome.

Trevor couldn't seem to get his feet underneath himself. He flapped and floundered in the huge landlord's clutches, his trainers skittering across the floor. He was shrieking like a baby, kicking and screaming.

'Shut it!' Alan boomed, and slapped him hard in

the face with his open fist. He hauled the suddenly limp, greasy-faced lout across the floor to the pub's small doorway. He literally threw him through it. 'You're barred!'

Tom was quiet now. He shook free of the last few restraining hands. His wig had fallen off and his real hair was a horseshoe of close-cropped grey around his head. His fists were still clenched, his face still red. Joseph could see him struggling to calm himself, gritting his teeth, holding his head down. He only looked up when the landlord lumbered over to him.

Alan said, 'Finish your drink, Tom. Give him time to move on, then you go too.'

Tom nodded slowly. The men began to move away, back to the bar or the dartboard, righting the few overturned tables and picking up the larger chunks of glass.

'I did warn you.'

Again Tom nodded. He still held his dignity in his firm stance, but his hands were no longer fists. He held the landlord's eyes in his. He looked nothing like a chastised little boy, but he knew there had been no honour in his outburst.

'Give yourself a couple of weeks. Go see your

lad and his missus. The grandkids could do with a visit from their grandad.' Alan put a slab of a hand on the old man's shoulder.

Tom didn't say a word. He walked over to where his wig lay like a little dead thing and picked it up. He stuffed it into his trouser pocket, but dark tufts still stuck out over the top. He came back over to the table where Don and Joseph were sitting. Don went to speak and Tom held up a hand to shush him. He ruffled Joseph's hair. 'Silly old fool,' he said quietly to himself. Then drained the last of his pint.

Chapter Five

Tom Beverly led the way. Don and Joseph walked with him along the dark country lane, carrying their rucksacks on their backs. Don walked slowly, carefully, the alcohol still thick in his head. Tom had invited them to stay the night at his house because Don was in no fit state to drive. And Joseph hated his father for it.

Joseph listened to the old man talk, and was grateful his father at least had the common sense to shut up and listen as well. Tom's outburst seemed to have sobered him up, or at least purged him of that hostility he'd had buried inside. He spoke quietly.

Don had tried to smile at his son, tried to throw an arm round the boy's shoulders, (either in buddiness or for support, Joseph wasn't sure) but the boy hadn't let him. He was embarrassed about having to accept Tom's charity because of his father's stupidity. The Land-Rover was still parked outside The Retreat. Don had tried to make a joke of it,

'Don't sprag on me to your mother,' he'd said.

It was an extremely dark night; the cloud was still thick and the moon and the stars were all hiding behind it. There were no streetlights. The hills rising up on either side of the road were black. There was a chill wind, but Joseph had his coat buttoned right up to his chin, his hands stuffed deep in his pockets, and at least it wasn't raining. The road wound in and out of the hills, rising and falling with their lower slopes. No traffic passed by in either direction.

The walk was only a short one. And in the fifteen or twenty minutes it took them to reach Tom Beverly's little farmhouse, he told them his first story:

'She wasn't mad. She wasn't even a fool. She was just old, that's all.

'She still had her own teeth, still looked a million dollars, and only needed her glasses for reading the newspapers – I swear the print's been getting smaller and smaller over the years. So she wasn't doing badly. She was lucky really . . . God, *I* was lucky really. To find a woman like her who could put up with my moods and my tantrums. When I think back . . .

'She deserved a little love at the end. And not just

from me. From some of them others as well. All too high and mighty for her in the end, though.

'The first time I saw her ... That day, I knew I'd ...

'She was a vision. Long dress with little blue flowers, tiny wrists and ankles, her hair all neat, but in a style much too old for her. And she had me fooled.

'I'd just finished my time in the army (missed the war by three years, but still had to do my time) and me and a friend, Johnny Lambert, we were back home and out on the town. We went to the new dance hall, The Globe; it'd only been open a few months and we'd bought new suits especially with our last army pay. I swear she looked older than nineteen. Twenty-five, I thought she was. At least twenty-five. And all night I kept on gearing myself up to ask her to dance, but things were so different back then. A lass of twenty-five was considered to be left on the shelf if she still wasn't married, so I kept thinking to myself that her feller would be somewhere close by. If I'd known the truth I would've saved myself a lot of heartache. I don't believe in love at first sight, that's for poets and their sort – and I don't really believe in them either. All I knew was that she was the prettiest girl I reckoned I'd ever seen.

'Johnny knew her though, she'd been at his school, he knew how old she really was. But he wasn't letting on to me because he'd decided that after the barrack-rooms mebbe she was the prettiest little thing he'd ever seen too. Whenever my back was turned he was there, and I didn't know a thing about it. Arranging to take her to the pictures right under my very nose. Always was too big for me to see what was under it, anyhow. But it just so happened that I bumped into her on the bus about a fortnight later. She sat down next to me, bold as you like, and started talking about Johnny. And the first chance I got I marched straight round to his house and gave him a mouthful. His mam was furious, me shouting in the front garden for all the neighbours to hear. Not that I cared. Couldn't care less. I let the whole street know what a little back-stabber she'd raised. Though I caught it off *my* mam when she found out what I'd done.

'It was only a few days after when I came up here to live with my grandad and learn how to shepherd, and I thought I'd never see her again. And you know, I didn't even know her name when I came, but she wrote to me. She told me she'd split up with Johnny and said she'd been told about my little fit of temper at the Lamberts'. She said she was actually quite flattered by it. She signed the letter Jane Burroughs, and it was in the neatest handwriting you've ever seen. She wanted to be a teacher you see, and thought good handwriting was important.

'So we wrote to each other, back and forth, keeping the postman busy. Every week became twice a week, then every other day. I don't know how I filled so many pieces of paper, my life certainly wasn't full of front-page news, living out in the middle of nowhere. And then she came all the way out here to see me. She came on the train when Becksall still had its little station and I took her for a walk in the hills. It was a glorious, sunny day; she was twice the vision she'd been in that tatty dance hall, and that was the day I fell in love with her. But from the very first time I'd met her I'd known I'd wanted to.

'She came to the farm as often as she could. And we were married within the year. Grandad was pushed into the small bedroom, poor old feller, but Jane looked after him well, and he always talked of her as his little angel. She was a wonderful cook, and a real generous one too, and I reckon she soon came to love looking after the two of us as much as we loved looking after her. They were the good times; I was a very happy man in those days. But back then I didn't realise what I'd made her do. I realise it now, and no matter how hard I wish, I know I can't ever change it. Jane never did become a teacher. I guess she was too busy with Grandad and me.

'And she *was* an angel, she really was, I truly believe that. But I reckon God was too blind to see it. He's not all-knowing, not like I was taught at Sunday school. If He was then He would've seen what she was and He wouldn't have put her through what He did. We did all the right things. We raised a family as best as we knew how, we helped neighbours and all that, and never asked anyone for anything we couldn't pay for in some way. If anyone should have gone through what she suffered it should have been me. I was the one with the temper; I was certainly no angel. But God was too blind and too stupid to realise He'd picked on the wrong one. Makes me think that mebbe I'm not the only silly old fool still hanging around.

'It was little things at first. She'd just forget where she'd put things. And we'd laugh about it, like the way we'd laugh about our creaking bones and my going bald. We weren't complaining, we were fairly settled in our old age. When my grandad had gone he'd left the farm and the land to us as he'd always promised. Our lad, Peter, he had his own family down in London, and we were happy to be on our own. We had peaceful years ahead of us. But she had a stroke. She recovered quickly the doctors said, always was strong like that, but those little things began to get bigger. And soon she'd be going into the village to buy groceries and forgetting exactly what it was she wanted. Or she'd cycle in on that old push-bike of hers and forget where she'd left it and have to come home in the village taxi.

'Everybody began to notice of course, and she started worrying that they'd all be talking about her behind her back. It happened again, her forgetting where she'd left her bike, and instead of getting the taxi and letting them all talk about her, she walked home. And it's a good four or five miles, you know. And it's a sixty-year-old lady I'm talking about. She was sobbing by the time she got home; her feet and legs hurting so bad, and I suppose the embarrassment of it all.

'I still can't believe how quickly all of this seemed to happen. It was as if we'd lived with the little things for years, but the big things all came within a few months, just after the stroke. I think back now to how I felt that day when she walked with me for the first time in the hills. We were young, falling in love, and somehow glorious. And I can't believe how we turned out in the end. The love never died, never will, but old age had washed away any of the glory left in us.

'People weren't talking about her behind her back of course, or at least not nastily, not at first. I got quite a few phone calls asking how she was that day, or if anyone could do anything for her. Especially from Katie Morgan at the Post Office, she was Jane's oldest friend round this way. It was that Trevor Toomey who started spreading the rumours. He's got a lot to answer for, that one. He'd once worked for me when he was a bairn, just doing odd jobs for me, tidying the leaves up or something. But I'd sacked him for thieving. Couldn't prove it, but I knew it was him. Mebbe that was why he said what he did. Or mebbe he's just filth through and through. He's the one that drives the village taxi now; his uncle passed the car and business on to him, and one of his main fares is the doctor. The doctor never did learn to drive, you see, they don't teach that at medical school. And when your patients are spread out as far and wide as his, you need some way of getting to them. And that was how Trevor Toomey got to know most of our business.

'I knew things were coming to an end when Jane began to forget my name and who I was. Some days she would treat me like a complete stranger. And she'd have funny turns, speaking nonsense, and crying or screaming for no reason anyone could see. I had the doctor almost living with us, I didn't know what else to do. But it also meant that Toomey was around a lot. The sheep were left to fend for themselves, I certainly didn't have time for them. And Toomey was returning to the village with some nice little stories, half made up in his own head.

'Now I'm not saying people believed all he was saying. I was still getting phone calls and offers of help, but I think his stories were getting to be more interesting than what really was happening, if you know what I mean. And I'm afraid there's very little excitement in a place like this. I know I didn't help matters, but I didn't know what he was saying to others in The Retreat or at the grocer's. I wouldn't let Jane into the village on her own any more and wouldn't let anybody come and visit her. I just didn't want anybody seeing her the way she was. I didn't want anybody thinking of her like that. And behind my back the rumours soon began to spread. Toomey gave them all some nice little bedtime stories, that's for sure.

'I used to watch her when she had her turns and think that things just couldn't get any worse for her. I used to think that surely she was suffering enough and that it was just impossible for her to suffer any more. But I was wrong. She had always fought against what was happening to her, and when she had her good days she'd be out in the garden or cleaning the house, not wasting her time, refusing to give in. Then all of a sudden she stopped her fighting. She was finally pushed over the edge. She stopped fighting and started trying to run away from it instead. I could see it in her eyes . . . And it broke my heart.

'It was exactly a week before she died. I woke up in the middle of the night to hear her screaming and crying, howling like a baby. She was worse than she'd ever been before. She was saying over and over that she'd seen it in the garden and that it was coming to get her. I had to call the doctor, she wouldn't take any of her pills from me. I couldn't control her, and I was so scared myself, at seeing her like that. So I had to call him. And Toomey drove him here.

'And of course, telling everybody is exactly what he did. Telling people stories about an old woman in a lot of pain, so they could mock her behind her back. He told them she was saying she'd seen the angel of death in her own backyard. He made her look like a mad woman. He's turned her into a freak now. A story for them all to tell each other in years to come. And I hope he rots in Hell for it. I hope God's eyes are *wide* open when he dies.

'As I said, this was only a week or so before she finally passed away, and she only had one clear patch before she went. But it was then that she told me what she'd seen.

'She'd gotten up in the middle of the night to get herself a glass of water, but when she was in the kitchen she'd forgotten exactly what it was she wanted. So she'd stood there, trying to fight it, trying to force herself to remember why she'd gotten out of bed. She'd been feeling really good for the few days before this and had almost felt in control of what was wrong with her. She thought that if she tried to hold it off then she'd be OK.

'She said she'd been standing at the sink, leaning on it with her eyes tight shut, trying to remember, hating herself for forgetting. She didn't know how long she'd been standing there, she said she might even have reached the point where she'd forgotten that she was trying to remember anything. But she got this strange sensation that she was being watched and she got scared to open her eyes. The sink is right in front of the window, and she said that standing there in the kitchen's bright lights she could feel goose bumps rising and a prickle at the back of her neck. The feeling got stronger and stronger as she realised she was in full view of anyone who was out there in the dark, looking in. And she got scared to open her eyes, because she didn't want to see who it was that was watching her.

'But she fought it like she'd fought everything else. She told herself not to be ridiculous, that it was all in her imagination. Who on earth was going to be in our back garden, out here in the middle of the night? And she forced herself to open her eyes. And she saw

58

another pair of eyes looking right back at her.

'She could see herself reflected in the window, but past that, through her reflection, she could see the eyes staring straight at her. They didn't move. They just looked at her. And she said it wasn't a man. She said, whatever it was in the back garden couldn't have been a man. The eyes were wide and yellow, watching her. They were low to the ground and didn't blink. They just stared at her. And that was when she started screaming. But of course, by the time I got to her it was long gone.

'And I've stood at that window long into the night in the weeks since. I've waited for it. And I know it keeps coming back, but I keep missing my chance. I know it finally pushed her over the edge. It stole my wife's life. And I'll stand there with my gun for as long as it takes. I'll get it, before it gets me.'

Tom's army-straight shoulders were stooped now; he looked tired. He looked as though he hadn't talked so much in years.

Joseph was cold, the walking seemed to have done little to warm him. The old man was quiet now and all Joseph could hear was the steady tramp of their feet and his father's heavy breathing. The hills themselves were silent. Against his will his eyes kept on glancing towards them. Their blackness seemed to be surrounding him, rising up and closing him in. Could something be watching them now?

He shivered and stared at his feet.

Chapter Six

The three of them turned off the road and headed up a steep and narrow track. Tom's farmhouse sat at the top of the rise and even in the dark Joseph thought that the old man and his home were ideally suited. They were both squat and quite stocky, both looked weather-beaten but still solid. And the farmhouse even had a thatched roof.

'Here he is. Here's the lad,' Tom said, as a collie dog appeared from out of the open front porch to greet his master. The old man smiled for the first time since his outburst at The Retreat. And it was a smile of genuine warmth, at the sight of his dog.

Joseph wasn't at all surprised to see the grey around the collie's muzzle and the slight, bandy limp it had as it walked. He was used to always being among young people; at school, at the youth club, in the park; his own generation. Apart from his parents and teachers (who still couldn't exactly be described as really old) he was usually only ever surrounded by the young. But now it felt as though the deeper and deeper he headed into the country, the older everything seemed to be getting. And of course, the hills were the oldest of all.

'You got bored and left me again, didn't you, eh?' Tom was saying to the collie as he fussed it gently. 'Well it won't be happening again for a while, lad. It looks like you're not the only old dog Lizzie's not going to be letting in any more.'

The dog obviously didn't understand a word Tom was saying, but it licked his hand and wagged its tail anyway, then turned and led them back up to the front porch where it had been waiting. It hadn't taken the slightest bit of interest in Don or Joseph.

The farmhouse was dusty but tidy inside. It reminded Joseph of his grandparents' house, mainly because of the amount of ornaments that clustered on shelves and sideboards everywhere. It seemed to him that the older someone became the more ornaments they accumulated, because nobody knew what on earth else to buy them for their birthday. So there was no wonder the little house was dusty too. He reckoned only the very bored or very house-proud would bother to find time to dust each and every individual nick-nack and porcelain ballerina. There were also several ash-trays on tables or windowsills, not that Joseph had seen Tom with a cigarette all evening. He thought maybe the old man's wife had smoked.

Once the lights were on and the three of them were beginning to warm up, conversation slowly began again. Don started it awkwardly by talking about the house, about how he'd always dreamed of living in a place like this, but he was still quite drunk and it was obvious he was struggling to talk sense. Tom didn't seem to mind however, he seemed to be pleased of the company. He showed them a photograph of his wife. Don said he thought she was beautiful, but Joseph knew he was only saying it because it was the polite thing to say. Joseph meant it though, and he would have said so too, if he'd been asked. She had the strong and elegant look of a headmistress, but the smile of your favourite dinner lady.

They sat at the kitchen table, waiting for the kettle to boil on the gas hob. Joseph wished Tom would pull down the blind, because he felt as though the window above the sink was staring at him like a huge, blank eye. It was leaded, sectioning off the darkness outside into neat little rectangles. He was sitting right in front of it and considered moving his chair so he had his back to it. He could just imagine . . . He tried to get the dog's attention by calling it, wanting to tickle its ears. But the collie wouldn't move from its master's side.

'What's he called?' Don asked, nodding at the dog, still wanting to keep the conversation on a light note. 'He looks as though he's about as old as the rest of us.'

'Aye, he's getting on a bit,' Tom said, 'aren't you, lad?' The dog looked up at him. 'He's called Cos,' Tom continued. 'It was my son, Peter, who chose it. He was about young Joseph's age when we got the lad here, and I told him he could choose. He was quite firm he wanted to call him Cos, even though the wife wanted him called Skipper, after his father. I asked him why he wanted to name him Cos, and Pete said, "Because I said so." It was his idea of a joke at my expense, I think. Whenever he wanted to do something and I said no, he'd ask me why and I'd say "Because I said so." '

Don laughed.

'Trying to get one up on his old dad, wasn't he, lad?' The dog lifted its muzzle to be stroked. Tom turned to Don. 'He's seen it too, you know.'

Don was confused. 'I'm sorry?'

'The lad, here.' Tom pointed at Cos. 'He's seen it out in the garden as well. Even chased it off once.'

Don and Joseph were silent. The window stared at them both from over the old man's shoulder.

'It was here the other night. The lad saw it, but couldn't wake me up in time. Lizzie'd been a bit too nice to me that night, hadn't she?' He scratched the old collie's head. He was still looking at the dog when he added. 'And you know something? I think I'm getting a bit fed up with the two of us waiting around for it to keep coming here. I'm beginning to reckon it's high time we went out there looking for it, instead. What d'you think of that, eh? D'you fancy a bit of a hunting trip, lad?'

The kettle hissed and whistled suddenly, as it boiled.

Don squirmed a little on his stool, as if it was uncomfortable for him to sit still.

Steam jetted out of the kettle's spout, pushing the whistle higher and higher in pitch.

Joseph stared at the dog. His eyes felt as if they were being pulled . . . But he refused to look at the black, blank window.

Tom stood up slowly and moved over to the hob where the kettle shrieked and steamed. Don cleared his throat and fidgeted on his seat again. He looked as though he was going to say something . . . then didn't. Tom used a tea towel with a garish map of the British Isles pictured on it to lift the kettle off the heat and kill its din. Joseph told himself he was being silly, ridiculous. But still wouldn't lift his eyes to look out of the window.

'Erm . . .' Don shuffled around a bit. He cleared his throat, shrugged. 'So . . . Erm . . .'

Joseph cringed inwardly. He was thinking, Don't ask. Just don't ask.

But Don had never been able to read his son's thoughts. 'What, you know . . . ? What exactly *is* it, do you think?'

Tom filled a chubby, white teapot, with blue flowers painted on the sides, from the kettle. 'It's a cat,' he said. And reached down three mugs from the cabinet above his head.

'A cat?' Don's tone was incredulous.

Tom turned and stared at the younger man. 'Aye. A cat,' he said. 'I don't know what Jane thought she saw, but I know it was a cat.' He was almost daring Don to disagree. 'A big cat. A wild cat.'

'What? Like a panther, or a puma, or something?'

'Mebbe. Wouldn't know the difference unless it had spots or stripes.'

'You've seen it yourself?'

'Only its backside as Cos ran it off into the hills. But I know what it is.'

There was a pause then. Don stopped his fidgeting and Tom watched the teapot while he waited for the tea to mash. Joseph was kind of hoping it would be the end of the conversation altogether. He felt childish for letting Tom's tale spook him, but he also felt a little embarrassment for the old man, who had obviously suffered because of his wife's death and was maybe letting the drink and the grief get to him, cloud his mind.

'I think I've heard about this kind of thing before,' Don said, suddenly. And now Joseph was the one to fidget uncomfortably in his seat. 'Yes,' Don nodded, 'I saw it on the news, but quite a while ago, now. There was a bit outcry about it. About these wild cats everybody claimed were roaming the countryside. It was in the papers and everything.' He clicked his fingers. 'What did they call it?' He pulled a face and looked at Joseph as he searched for the name. But Joseph wouldn't help him. 'The Beast of Bodmin Moor,' he exclaimed, triumphantly. 'That was it. It attacked some woman down south, near Dartmoor. And there was one photographed near Durham. That was a puma.'

Tom was silent as he poured the tea.

'You must have heard of them,' Don told him, sounding excited. 'The papers were full of them, it was either big cats or crop circles.'

Tom gave them a mug each. Joseph mumbled his thanks, wishing his father would shut up and drink his tea. But Don was far too excited. 'ABCs they called them. Alien Big Cats. They were crawling out of the woodwork if you believed all the reports. It was claimed they'd escaped from zoos or circuses, but had never been reported because of the stink it would cause.'

Tom sat down again. 'I don't care what it is or how it got here.' His unsteady voice betrayed his anger. 'It killed my wife. She could've got better.'

'And you're quite serious about hunting the thing down?' Don asked.

'It killed my wife,' Tom repeated.

Don ignored his mug of tea. He leaned forwards across the table. 'We'll go with you,' he said quickly. He turned to Joseph. 'What do you think? Chance of a lifetime if we see it. And far better than any fishing trip, eh? Far more exciting, eh?'

Joseph didn't answer. He was still staring at the dog who, he now realised, was staring out of the kitchen window and into the night.

Chapter Seven

A dog; loud. Each bark a slap that jarred the boy from his sleep. Hurried footsteps in the hall, running past the bedroom door. He opened his eyes but the darkness was complete. He stayed quiet, he wouldn't move. What time is it? The dog raging. A man's voice – his father's voice: 'Is that it? Is it out there?' Excited, nervous. The barks so sharp in the darkness. Tom's voice then, but the words were lost. Running through the farmhouse. A door was opened. A boom, and the night shook. A gun? The harsh barks echoed as the dog ran into the night, trailing away, quietening, calming.

But when Joseph woke the next morning, it could all so easily have been a dream.

The sound of the Land-Rover pulling up in front of the farmhouse woke Joseph at around eight thirty; his father must have risen early to fetch it from outside The Retreat. Joseph had slept quite well, considering. The bed had been soft and warm, and the clean sheets had felt crisp and fresh. He lay quietly for a few minutes, thinking about what could have been a dream. He mulled over in his mind all that had been said the previous night. He told himself he didn't believe in it. Pumas and cougars and panthers roaming the countryside. Circus escapees. A wild cat in the hills. Of course he didn't believe it. But . . .

His father knocked lightly on the door to ask if he wanted breakfast.

He washed and dressed quickly then joined the two men in the kitchen. He looked briefly for the old collie but it wasn't there. Tom was cooking toast under the grill, while Don was standing by the sink, mug of tea in hand, staring out of the window. Joseph had a small hope that everything his father had said last night had been induced by the Old Peculier, or at least would look preposterous in the sober light of day.

Don smiled at him, took a sip of his tea. 'Hiya, Joe. Sleep well?'

Joseph shrugged non-committally. He was disappointed to see him looking remarkably spry and cheery

71

considering the amount he'd had to drink the night before.

Don stepped away from the window. 'There was a bit of a commotion last night; I wasn't sure if we'd woken you or not. And you're going to need all your energy today,' he said with a grin. 'We've got a bit of a walk ahead of us. Tom and I have already . . .'

Joseph interrupted him. 'Is it OK if I phone Mum?'

His father's grin slipped. But only for a second. 'I guess so,' he said, 'I'll just nip to the Land-Rover and fetch my mobile.'

'Phone's in the front room,' Tom said, without turning around.

Don was slightly taken aback, but Joseph ignored him by saying thank you and leaving the two men in the kitchen.

It was an old-fashioned telephone, sitting with an empty glass vase on a small wooden table. It was big and chunky and green with a dial instead of buttons. Joseph's fingers didn't quite fit into the holes on the dial and it seemed to take an age to spin each particular number, then let it return before he could spin the next. His mother hadn't even had time to answer before his father appeared in the room behind him and hovered near the door.

'Hi, Mum. It's me.'

'Joseph.' She sounded a little surprised. He imagined her sitting at the telephone table in the hall, wearing the blue towelling dressing-gown he'd bought her for her birthday. It was too small for her, but she always wore it just the same. 'I wasn't expecting to hear from you. Are you having a good time? Shouldn't you be lost in the wilderness somewhere?'

He guessed it was a double-barrelled question. It very probably also meant, Is everything OK? so he answered his interpretation of the question with a Yes.

His father was still hovering, no doubt worried that Joseph was going to sprag on him for getting drunk. And Joseph did consider telling his mother. Once again he felt that slight thrill at knowing he held some sort of power over the weekend. Knowing that no matter how much control his father might have over him and his life usually, right now it wasn't quite complete.

'How's your dad?' She was still looking for the reason behind his call.

'All right.'

'You two aren't arguing, are you?'

'No.'

She was quiet then, the distance between them buzzing softly down the line. She'd run out of immediate possibilities for the surprise call and was trying hard to think of some more.

'Did the Land-Rover get you there safely?'

'Oh, yeah. Fine.' To tell the truth, Joseph wasn't all that sure why he'd wanted to phone her either. Surely it wasn't *just* to make his father squirm?

He felt suddenly awkward now. He realised he had nothing to say.

His mother asked, 'Have you caught many fish yet?'

And Joseph said, 'Oh, we're not going fishing any more. We're going hunting for pumas with this old man Dad met in the pub last night.' Then he handed the phone to his father to let him explain.

He moved back through to the kitchen, feeling a little childish. But then a certain smugness filled his head. He knew his father was going to have to do some pretty fast talking to get out of that one. His mother was one of those anxious ladies; she flapped.

She had never let him ride too high on the swings, or play football with the older boys. A sniffle was a cold, a graze needed a bandage. It was only when he'd started at the secondary school that she had been forced to succumb to letting him off the leash. But even so, she still insisted he wore a cycle helmet when none of the other lads at school did, and would not let him out of the house until she knew exactly where and with whom he was going. And every now and again Joseph liked to torture her. There had been plenty of times when he'd come home long after he'd said he'd be back, even when there was no real reason for him to be late at all.

Back in the kitchen, Cos had appeared. He was sitting at Tom's feet and the old man was feeding him toast from the table. Joseph noticed the dog's paws were caked with mud. He sat down and Tom pushed a plate piled high with toast across the table towards him.

'Just done,' the old man told him.

Joseph ate his toast in silence, wondering what the conversation between his parents was like. He wished he'd maybe hung around a bit longer to hear what was said. Although he knew his father would eventually talk his mother round, he always did. He always got his own way.

Tom talked quietly to Cos as he fed him, the dog seeming to pay close attention, watching his master's face. Joseph watched too. Once again he felt the need to be accepted by the old man. He wanted to tell him about school. He wanted to tell him about his friends, about the lads he played football with, down at the park, about the ones he went on bike rides with. He wanted to tell him about Sarah Beechwood, the girl he'd fallen in love with, who he wished he had the courage to talk to. She had long, long, brown hair which she wore in a plait and big, blue eyes. Tom looked like someone who would listen. Joseph wanted to tell him about his father. He wanted to tell him about his mother, and was so close to inviting him to speak to her on the phone. He wanted to tell him about his drawings, too. Maybe them most of all. Because drawing was what he was best at, and his covers were what he was most proud of.

Joseph had always read, he enjoyed reading; he always had one book or another on the go. But after he'd finished reading the book he nearly always found that the cover was no good. More often than not it was obvious the artist or designer, or whoever, hadn't bothered to read it themselves, and therefore the picture on the outside simply didn't suit the story on the inside. So Joseph redrew them. He redrew them how they should have been done in the first place. His bedroom walls and wardrobe doors were heavy with his pictures. He was redrawing the front cover to *Watership Down* at the moment, he couldn't believe how wrong they'd got it. It made it look like a girls' book, with all the rabbits eating daisies in the long grass. Joseph was determined to draw something which reflected the violence and cruelty he'd found within its pages. And he was good at drawing too, he was top of the class – or at least had been. There was no money in drawing pictures, so his father had said that there was no point in taking an exam in it. He'd been told he had to do chemistry now, instead. He hated chemistry; he was going to fail for sure. But only because he wanted to. Only because it would annoy his father.

He hated the way his father controlled his life. Even when his parents had been separated Don seemed to have been pulling his strings. It was yet another reason not to want the man living back home again; it would surely make things worse. Since his father had been back Joseph had felt as if he had a little, telescopic aerial sticking out of his backside and his father was holding the remote control, tweaking the knobs to steer him this way and that.

He ate his toast, sucking the hot butter from his fingertips, watching Tom and Cos. He wished he'd brought some of his drawings with him. He wanted to show them to Tom, tell him all about them. Tom would understand. He wanted to tell him all about himself. He thought about the old man's wife, about how much he must have loved her . . .

'I believe in it,' he said suddenly. He kind of blurted the words out before he realised what he was saying, or even really knowing why he'd said it.

Tom looked up at him. His brows furrowed into a question mark.

'The cat,' Joseph said, embarrassed now, but feeling as though he had to explain. 'I believe in the cat.' He gestured tentatively at the window above the sink. 'Being out there.'

The old man grunted, nodded. 'So you should,' he said. 'So you should.'

Chapter Eight

The morning sun was bright but chill like a winter's day. The sky was empty. Yesterday's cloud had moved on or disappeared, and the hills rolled away underneath the pale blue for as far as the eye could see. They looked blank, lifeless, not even a tree to break the view. The four of them had set off walking just after ten that morning. Cos had led the way up into the hills behind Tom Beverly's farmhouse. Don and Joseph carried their rucksacks, and apart from his own pack, Tom had a rough, canvas bag thrown over one shoulder. Joseph knew what the old man was carrying in the bag, he'd seen him cleaning the shotgun earlier. The old man was bald this morning, he'd left his wig sitting next to an empty milk bottle on the kitchen windowsill. He was wearing a dark, heavy coat and a huge pair of hiking boots.

There was a strong breeze which ran in ripples through the heather and long grass. They followed the irregular curves of the hills, not yet venturing too high into them. Joseph hoped the dog knew where it was going, he couldn't remember anybody telling it their exact destination.

They stood for a moment to take a look around themselves. The farmhouse was lost a long way behind the hills now.

'That's Abraham's Height,' Tom said, pointing away from the sun at the highest peak they could see. 'Probably the tallest around here. And running down from there, those smaller peaks, they're what my grandad always called, His Teeth. Abraham's, I suppose. See the way the rocks stick up kind of straight?' Don was nodding his head, taking it all in. 'Behind them is The Leap. That's where you would have been fishing.'

'This is beautiful,' Don said, for the umpteenth time. He had bought a new rucksack and cagoule especially for the weekend, and their bright greens and yellows were in matching slashes and stripes. He held his arms wide to encompass it all, everything, the whole lot. 'Now *this* is my type of country.' He turned to look at his son. 'What do you think, Joe? Do you reckon I could persuade your mother to come and live up here?' There was no talk of what they were supposed to be hunting. And that seemed some-how quite odd to Joseph.

They had to clamber over some fallen rocks and push through tangled clumps of heavy, ragged bracken to be able to make their way down into a slight gully with a gentler slope to climb. Joseph was a step or two behind Tom and his father, and picked up his pace a little so that he was able to walk beside them. He didn't like the way Don had all of the old man's attention.

They climbed high over one hill with the breeze beginning to bite near the top. Streaks of cloud had appeared. They moved slowly and silently across the sky, growing thinner as they sailed by against the pale blue, trailing out, becoming stranded wisps, then finally disappearing altogether as they passed overhead. The view was magnificent. Joseph looked all around, turning a full 360 degrees, and could not see a single thing that was man-made. There were no houses, no telephone lines, no electricity pylons, only the countryside as it rolled away. On top of them all, looking down into the narrow valleys, the hills didn't seem quite so bad. But Joseph knew that standing at the bottom and feeling them all around you was a completely different experience.

They followed Cos down the other side to cross a small brook, tumbling and churning against itself and the jagged path it had cut through the hillside. 'We're off my land now,' Tom told them as he half-stepped, half-jumped across at the narrowest part.

'Quite a back garden you've got there,' Don said, and Tom smiled. They'd been walking for a little over two hours. 'This friend of yours,' Don continued, 'did you let him know we were coming?'

Tom shook his head. 'Art doesn't have a phone,' he said. 'Doesn't like them either, won't have one in the house. He says it's no good talking to people when you can't see them, because then you can't tell if they're lying or not.'

Don nodded, but didn't say anything. Joseph grinned to himself. He knew his father conducted most of his business over the phone. He guessed he probably had his mobile tucked away somewhere in that new rucksack of his, too.

They began to follow the path that the brook was taking along the hillside. Tom's friend was a man called Art Hooper, another retired sheep-farmer. Tom said that for years Art had claimed there was something roaming the hills around Becksall and killing his sheep. Tom thought that if anyone could point them in the direction of the cat, then it was him.

Chapter Nine

'Art isn't too fond of company,' Tom told them. 'It'd be best if I went to see him first, see what his mood's like. He's got a habit of letting his dog out when there's visitors.'

Neither Don nor Joseph argued. They watched as he made his way up to the cottage's front door, and listened to him trying to shout above the threatening barks of what sounded like a rather large dog. Joseph didn't think it was too comforting to notice that Cos hadn't followed him either. The old collie stood a little way from the boy and his father, keeping a wary eye on his master's every move, but not attempting to get any closer. Eventually Tom let himself in through the front door and closed it quickly behind him, leaving the others waiting expectantly outside. The barking took another few minutes to quieten, however.

Art Hooper lived by the side of the noisy, rushing brook, deep down in the valley. A path led the way to his cottage, but no road. Joseph remembered thinking last night that Tom looked kind of similar to his farmhouse, and if the same applied to Art Hooper, then the man had to be ancient, ugly and barely able to stand by himself. There was a small, dense wood and the bent little house was standing right on the very edge of the trees – but only just. The trees were the first ones Joseph had seen in the hills, the rest of the countryside being too open to the harsh wind for them to get a strong root-hold, and the scene could have made a pretty little oasis amongst the bleak downs and fells if it hadn't been for the decrepit cottage.

Half of the chimney had crumbled away; the fallen bricks were either scattered across the battered slate roof or formed debris in the garden at the front of the cottage. The guttering had come away from the outside wall and the drainpipe looked as though it was reaching out, trying to grab a hold of anyone foolhardy enough to venture too near. There was a wooden shed to the left of the cottage, but that had no roof and no door, although surprisingly the window remained intact. The garden itself, or at least what had been the garden, was a mass of weeds and thistles. There was an old, rusted-red bicycle planted in amongst the havoc of foliage, but it hadn't grown any new wheels just yet.

'He sounds like a bit of a character, doesn't he, this friend of Tom's?' Don said.

Joseph shrugged.

'Must be the solitude,' his father told him.

They stood quietly for a moment, watching the outside of the cottage. Then Don said, 'I didn't think what you did this morning was very fair, by the way.'

Joseph didn't answer, and he wouldn't meet his father's gaze.

'Apart from putting me in a difficult situation with your mother, she's now going to be sitting at home fretting for the rest of the weekend. You know what she's like.'

Joseph shrugged.

'Don't you want to be here? Is that it?'

Again the boy shrugged.

His father dropped his eyes briefly. Then lifted them back up to Art Hooper's cottage. 'Something's going to have to change between us, Joseph. You realise that, don't you? Something's definitely got to alter.'

Joseph bit his lip, literally, to stop himself from

saying all the things he knew were bubbling away under the surface. He knew things had to change. As a matter of fact he wanted things to change. But in his eyes it was his father who should be making the changes, not him. He'd not asked the man to come back. He'd not asked him to go away in the first place. He didn't know how his father dared to talk about being fair.

They waited for maybe as long as a quarter of an hour before Tom appeared at the door again. On seeing his master, Cos immediately trotted over towards him; it was obvious they'd worked out this routine before. Tom waved Don and Joseph to come over too.

'Just mind what you say,' Tom warned them both when they got to the front door. 'And give him this,' he said, pushing a small pouch of Golden Virginia tobacco into Don's hand. Then he stepped back into the dim cottage, leaving the door open for them to follow.

The hallway smelled of a mixture of dog and cigarettes; the wallpaper was peeling in places, but the cottage wasn't as dirty on the inside as its outside suggested. But then it was obvious Art Hooper wasn't exactly house-proud either. Joseph was nervous. He wasn't sure why. He told himself it was because of the dog. He could hear it snarling behind a closed door at the end of the hall. Cos walked in front of them but ignored the sound.

Tom led them into a cramped, musty room with an old-fashioned radio turned low, people talking, no music. The room was bare; there were no ornaments collecting dust anywhere, just a couple of empty shelves. The radio was sitting on a wide mantelpiece above a cold fireplace heaped with black ash. And above the mantelpiece was a portrait of a hunting man and his dog, similar to the one hanging in The Retreat. This was the room's sole decoration. Art Hooper was sitting in a massive armchair with a pattern of faded flowers covering the worn fabric. He let Cos lick his hand and he tickled the dog's ears. He was ancient, ugly and certainly looked as though he was barely able to stand by himself.

Joseph remembered his thoughts last night about everything seeming to be so old. Art Hooper had to be one of the oldest. He looked old enough to be Tom Beverly's grandfather. His brow looked like a scrunched-up paper bag, all wrinkles and furrows.

The few strands of hair he had were white and wiry. He looked as old as the hills.

Art eyed the father and son with an open suspicion, but gestured for them to sit down anyway. Joseph sat in another faded armchair, and was almost swallowed whole by the thing, while Don sat tentatively on a wooden chair which trembled dangerously under his weight. Tom remained standing. But suddenly Don was on his feet again. He offered the old man the tobacco.

'I, erm . . .' He cleared his throat. 'I thought you'd like this,' he said.

Art Hooper took it slowly, almost lazily. He turned to Tom, and in a voice which literally creaked, he said, 'My favourite. How ever did you guess?' His leathery face smiled at his friend, and Joseph half-expected to hear his skin creak too.

Don sat back down again awkwardly on the fragile chair, looking embarrassed. Joseph found himself thinking about tribal chiefs, about old Red Indians who insisted on gifts from the palefaces. In fact, the more he thought about it, the more Art Hooper reminded him of some kind of shaman or witch doctor.

Tom went to speak, but Art Hooper held up a

bony hand to shush him. 'Let me have a cigarette first,' he said in that worn voice of his. He pulled a crumpled packet of Swan papers from out of his pocket and proceeded to use the tobacco Don had given him to slowly, painstakingly, roll the thinnest cigarette Joseph had ever seen. The radio noised in the background. Art offered the cigarette to Tom, who shook his head. 'Still given up?'

Tom nodded. 'Not smoked since Jane passed on,' he said quietly.

Art Hooper smiled, but not nastily. 'Aye, and maybe she's still able to appreciate that you have.' He took a small disposable lighter from out of another pocket and, holding the home-made cigarette between his thumb and first finger, touched the flame gently to one end. 'Though I'm sure she'd've appreciated it more if you'd done so when she first asked.' The paper and the tobacco were gently smouldering and he lifted the cigarette to his mouth. But to Joseph's surprise he put it between his lips the wrong way round. He sucked hard on the burning end, then blew the smoke out through his nose.

Joseph must have been staring because Art Hooper smiled at him. 'Best way to keep it lit,' he told the boy. The cigarette was still held in his lips and he spoke out of the corner of his mouth, tiny trails of smoke escaping with every word. 'When you're up in them hills and the rain's all over you, you still want to enjoy a cigarette, don't you? This's the best way I know how,' he said. He laughed his broken laugh again. 'I'm damned if I can taste half of what I eat, though.' He hadn't bothered to offer the cigarette to Don or Joseph.

And Tom hadn't bothered to introduce them. He waited for the older man to have a few puffs on his cigarette, then said, 'It was at my place again, last night. Not that I could find any tracks from the thing this morning.'

Art Hooper said nothing. Smoke came out of his nose. Joseph wondered where on earth the ash was going. He wondered if his tongue looked like the cold fireplace.

'I know you've seen it too,' Tom continued, 'you've talked to me about it before. I just never . . .'

'You say you're hunting it,' the older man interrupted him. 'You, and a boy, and the man in his fancy raincoat.' He didn't attempt to hide the scorn in his weary voice. Joseph felt his father flinch slightly, then felt himself blush. 'Listen to yourself, Tom. Can you hear what you're saying?' He blew hard down his nose and his weathered face was hidden behind a veil of smoke.

'I would be here on my own, just the same,' Tom told him.

Art Hooper gave a small gesture which could have been a shrug.

'I just want you to tell me where you've seen it, Art. I came here for that one favour. Nothing else.'

'You want some kind of revenge, don't you? Am I right? And the nice man here, I dare say he just wants a touch of adventure. City life getting a bit dull. What's the boy want?' Art Hooper turned his dark eyes to look at Joseph, and the boy physically shrank in his gaze. 'What d'you want? Why're you here?'

Joseph didn't answer, he couldn't. He stared at the old man, unable to take his eyes from the ancient face. He wouldn't have been able to say anything even if he'd had an answer.

'Got yourself dragged along, I guess,' Art Hooper said. 'Did your dad tell you it'd make a man of you?' He shook his head slowly. 'And you're the one with the most to lose. These men should know better. You'll be the one to suffer.' He sounded angry. His voice was no longer creaking, it was grinding against each and every word.

'Look, Art . . .'

The older man turned his glass-hard eyes back on Tom. 'I see your gun, Tom Beverly. I know you mean to kill it.'

Tom nodded. He was standing firm against this man the same as he had against the landlord of The Retreat. His shoulders were square. 'Aye. I mean to kill it.'

'Not that you will.'

'Tell me where I can find it and I'll kill it.'

Art Hooper laughed, the sound sharper than before, almost spiteful. Smoke poured out of his mouth and the laugh gurgled in his throat, choking him, and he coughed harshly against a clenched, bony fist. It got worse and he doubled up in his armchair. The sound of his cough was a hacking, deep down in his chest. Tom stepped forward to help him, but Art held up a hand to keep his friend at bay. Then put the hand to his chest as though trying to hold the cough down. Joseph became absurdly frightened the old man was going to die. But he reached for a glass ash-tray from the floor at the side of his armchair and spat the cigarette into it. Phlegm stretched in a glistening trail from his lips to the dead butt, and he brushed it away quickly with the back of his hand. The coughing slowly subsided and the old man was left with tears in his eyes. The anonymous radio voices filled the silence.

Art Hooper was grimacing, he looked in pain. He took a deep breath, setting himself for another bout of coughing which never came. He wiped the back of his wizened hand across his lips again and said, 'Why d'you think you don't find tracks, Tom? Why d'you think your dog can't catch it?' He stared hard into his friend's face. His body was trembling with tiny shivers. 'Why d'you think it scared Janey so damn bad when she saw it face to face?' His dark, wet eyes were pin-pricks as they stared at Tom. 'You *can't* kill it, that's why. You hear what I'm saying?'

Tom shook his head. 'Art, I . . .'

'You hear me, Tom Beverly. That thing's not natural. It's not meant to *be*.' He was leaning forwards in his hoary armchair, his hands gripping the arm-rests, sharp knuckles poking up against his white skin. 'I've seen it. I've seen it up real close, and I've felt it. You listening to what I'm saying?'

Again Tom shook his head. 'Tell me where to find it, Art. And I'll leave you be.'

Art Hooper slowly dropped his eyes; he was breathing hard through his nose. He leaned back in his chair again. His face relaxed in stages. He reached for another Swan paper and his pouch of Golden Virginia.

'It's all I'm asking. You can wash your hands from here.'

The old man nodded. He didn't look up from his task of rolling a fresh cigarette. 'It's where most devils can be found,' he said.

Tom nodded. Either a sharp nod of thanks or a quick nod of agreement, Joseph wasn't sure. He just knew he was thankful when Tom gestured for him and his father to leave the room, and they were both quick to their feet to follow him into the hallway in silence.

'Devils're easy to find when you go looking,' Art Hooper told both the empty room and the voices from the radio. 'Might even be waiting for you.'

Chapter Ten

Cloud shadows sailed smoothly by, racing them back up into the hills, and winning. They were virtually retracing their steps, walking against the flow of the noisy brook; Tom and Cos were leading the way, Don and Joseph a few steps behind. They walked in silence. Something was gnawing at Joseph's gut. But he told himself it wasn't Art Hooper's words. He felt as if the wizened old man was standing at his window watching them, those dark eyes pricking at the back of his neck. He was glad when a rise took them out of sight of the crumbling cottage at the edge of the trees.

'Must be the solitude,' Don said.

Tom didn't answer.

So Don quickened his pace to catch up with him. 'I said, it must be the solitude. Addled his mind.'

'I know what you said.'

Don nodded. 'Oh. Right.' He tried a different tack. 'So where are we headed, then? Where abouts do your local *devils* hang out?'

'The Leap.' The canvas bag which held his shot-gun jogged against Tom's shoulder.

'Hey, great. We'll get to see it after all,' Don said cheerfully.

'It'll take us a good few hours to walk,' Tom told him, his tone harsh. 'So best save your energy.'

Don took this as a signal to keep quiet, and reluctantly did so. He pulled on the shoulder straps of his flashy rucksack, hefting it up higher on his shoulders, and dropped back to walk beside his son. He offered the boy a smile.

Joseph pretended not to see it. He was thinking about Art Hooper's words. Maybe his father was right, maybe the old man was mad. It was even possible he was just trying to scare them for the sheer hell of it, he told himself. An old man taking the mick and getting the last few kicks he could. Joseph didn't believe in ghosts, so he certainly didn't believe in devils and demons and things. But the old man's words wouldn't leave him. Exactly what did Art Hooper mean by saying he had the most to lose? And he found himself unwillingly thinking about the horoscope his father had forced him into reading. He tried to remember what it had said. The line about something looming on his horizon, about something not going away of its own accord was all he could recall. So he urged himself to sneer.

It was this place, he told himself: these hills. No wonder he was letting himself feel spooked when he was wandering around in the middle of these hills. The higher they climbed, the more sparse and inhospitable the land became, the sharper the bite of the wind. He felt foolish now. He remembered Art Hooper's scorn at their little hunting party and realised just how judicious the old man had been. He felt like a little kid playing at *The X-Files*. No wonder the old man had said Tom and his father should know better.

The afternoon wore on, and they continued to walk in silence. Joseph was tiring now. He couldn't tell which was heavier, his rucksack or his boots. He'd lost count of how many hills they'd climbed; they all seemed to go on for ever. He'd expected them to be round at the top, like the way he'd always imagined hills to be, like the way he'd always drawn them. But they were all surprisingly flat, more like plateaux. They were small islands of grass in the sky, windblown and isolated from the next. They'd moved far from Tom or Art Hooper's land now, and sheep roamed freely among the hills. The animals stayed close together in loose huddles, their wool a dirty white, bleating every so often as if whining at one another. They never let the walkers come close to them, the small groups moving out of their way almost like a single, mewling creature with dozens of legs.

They stopped for something to eat when they reached His Teeth. It was just after four in the afternoon and Joseph was grateful for the rest. He didn't think he'd ever walked quite so far in his life before. Don looked tired too, but he hadn't said anything. And Joseph wasn't about to be the first one to complain.

The actual 'Teeth' themselves looked nothing like real teeth at all when they were close to. They were different from most of the other hills around them because they were more rock and cliff-face than grassy plateaux but it was only viewing them from a distance which gave them any kind of pattern or configuration. Abraham's Height was still a long way off, but was still the highest peak. When Tom had first pointed it out that morning it had looked as though the Height and His Teeth were right next to each other, as though you could reach out from one to touch the other, but once again it had been the hills playing tricks.

Distance and perspective both had a hand in confusing and disorientating.

They tried to shelter from the chill wind on a slope which shielded them against the strongest of its gusts. Joseph slumped down into the long grass, immediately pushing his rucksack off his back and away behind him. He slowly sucked in his breath as the relief from his sore feet rose up through the rest of his body. Don dropped down the same, just as happy to let his backside take the weight. But Tom merely crouched on his haunches and tickled Cos's ears when the old collie trotted over to sit in the grass next to him. Even the dog was breathing heavier than his master. His long pink tongue lolled out of his grey mouth as if he was trying to lap in an extra breath or two. Joseph reckoned that whenever Tom turned to Cos and said, 'walkies', he certainly meant it.

Don had made sandwiches that morning, and he passed them around with a couple of apples. He had a few cartons of soft drink which he'd brought for the fishing trip, and he offered one to Tom.

'How far from The Leap would you say we are?' he asked. He chose his words carefully, still unsure of the old man's mood.

'Mebbe another couple of hours,' Tom said, squirting the orange juice into his mouth, rather than bothering to suck it through the little plastic straw. 'I don't mean to be pushing you, but I think it's best we get there before dark.'

Don shrugged. 'That's OK. I reckon we both could do with the exercise, eh, Joe?' He took a bite of his apple, then grinned. 'Just, next time you want to go for a walk, let's go for one in the Land-Rover, agreed?'

Tom didn't reply, but his face conceded a smile.

They rested for a little over half an hour, a group of suspicious sheep keeping a discreet distance further up the slope, eating the grass with a wary eye on the trespassers. They would have stayed a while longer if the wind hadn't picked up. Cos's fur rippled like the grass and heather around them. Joseph dug his hands deep into his pockets, trying to huddle down inside his coat. The biting wind had spiteful teeth.

When they set off walking again, Don managed to keep a conversation going, trying to relieve the morbid silence which had hung over them earlier. He pointed out the buzzards he spotted circling high in the sky, and the lone tree which the wind had allowed to grow, but had twisted and bent in recompense. He also pointed out the dead sheep.

They had to clamber down into a small ravine of rocks and bushes to get to it, slipping slightly on the grass, treading carefully over the uneven ground. The carcass was half-in, half-out of a tangled gorse bush. It looked like a dirty, rumpled blanket that had been tossed carelessly to one side. The black head was crooked on its neck, its flat teeth were bared in death. The wool was sticky, spiked, as if gelled with blood; some of the gorse was tangled up with it. Tom kicked it over with his boot. And the animal had been opened up from front legs to back legs. The flesh was tattered, ripped open, the bones picked clean. It was a red, shiny skeleton in a dirty coat.

Don asked, 'Do you think it was . . . ?'

And Tom nodded.

'Could it have been a fox? Could a fox do this?'

Tom shrugged. 'Mebbe. But I doubt it.' He lifted his eyes to stare out across the hills. 'We're close,' he told them. 'Aye, we're very close.'

Chapter Eleven

They had reached The Leap a little before dusk, and Don had asked how the narrow valley had come by its name. Tom had said it was an old story.

The sky was darkening. The sun was leaving the day in a blood-red wash, but Joseph couldn't remember whether it was meant to signify shepherd's delight or warning. He watched the red glow slip slowly behind Abraham's Height and listened to Tom talk. They were going to wait until morning before they ventured down into the narrow valley. Don had set up the tent in the lee of some rocks which shielded the tent from the wind on three sides. Joseph thought they looked like massive Lego blocks which had been chewed and bitten at the edges by some enormous infant. Tom said he'd sometimes used the natural shelter himself when he'd been forced to spend nights up here in the hills. Joseph didn't like being so close to The Leap, to where the cat was supposed to roam, but the protection from the spiteful wind was welcome.

Tom had built a fire. They ate chicken legs (charred by the fire on the outside but still cold in the middle) and chunks of crusty bread. The old man stared into the flames as he spoke, his canvas bag across his knees, held in both hands, talking quietly as he told them his second story:

'My grandad was the first one to tell me the story. And I suppose it's one of those that's been passed down through the generations like that all the way along. I suppose it's what you'd call folklore round these parts.

'Anyways, in the olden times, and I'm talking way back before my years, before my grandad's too, there didn't used to be a Becksall. The village itself, I mean. There were just two farms in these parts, and both of them sitting on the north side of the hills, out past where Art Hooper's place is now. One of them's still standing to this day, a man called Henry Adams lives there, but I don't think his was the family that had it back in the times when I'm talking about. And there was a little chapel, which the two farmers had built between them, slap-bang in the middle of their two properties, and which their families shared on a Sunday.

'They built it on the side of a hill, overlooking the two properties, if you like. It took them exactly one year from when the first stone was laid to that Sunday when the two families met to worship within its walls for the first time. They had help in the building of it from the occasional traveller passing through the hills, who would lend a hand for a warm bed and a hearty meal, and they saw it as God's doing when carpenters or stonemasons were the ones passing through. But every member of the two families had a part in the building, right down to the youngest, who picked fresh flowers to decorate the altar. They even had a bell brought all the way from Lincoln for the little tower, no expense spared. They had a cobbled pathway leading up the hillside right to the front door, a cluster of carved angels greeting you as soon as you stepped inside, and a stained-glass window above the altar – a picture of Jesus Himself, that caught the sunlight and bathed the people in glorious reds and greens and blues as they prayed. When it was all eventually finished, after that year of hard work, it's said that it was one of the prettiest little buildings you were ever likely to see.

'The farmers welcomed all visitors there. The

wayfarers who passed through the hills were no longer asked to lend a hand in the building of the chapel, but were all invited to worship with the families instead. Now and again a pilgrim would come by, maybe on their way to York, and some of them were preachers or ministers themselves, and they'd bless the little chapel for the families, giving it God's seal of approval, if you like. Word spread, of course. People began telling stories about the beautiful chapel tucked away in the hills, an "oasis of faith" it was called, and some even began making pilgrimages to the chapel itself.

'Aye, word spread far and wide. Travellers from as far away as London, Newcastle and even Ireland had all heard tell of the farmers and their little chapel. Word spread so far in fact, that even the devil himself got to hear about it. And he was jealous. He was jealous of how pretty the little chapel was, of how all he could hear from up and down the land were people talking about it. About how even in the devil's own country of bleak and desolate hills, God had found a foothold. And he set about to change it.

'He brought wolves at night to roam around the farmers' cottages, baying at the moon and clawing at the doors. He peed in their wells and soiled in their grain. He spread disease through one farmer's live-stock, and gave the second a stillborn child with no eyes. But the farmers wouldn't back down. They knew the devil was only free to walk the earth at night and so spent their days praying in the chapel, but kept their families locked behind heavy doors as soon as it got dark. They hung silver crosses and herbs with healing powers on their walls, and buried written prayers under their doorsteps.

'The fight between the devil and the farmers went on for over a month, and their families were starving and their livestock dying, but it seemed God was listening and was ready to reward their faith, because it just so happened that the next wanderer to be travelling through the hills was a preacher. He was a young man, a handsome man so the story goes, riding a beautiful, chestnut horse. And although he may only have been young, his faith was strong and true. The farmers begged him for help and he told them he would stay in the chapel; he would pray all day long, and he would pray all night long, until he had laid enough blessings in the walls that the devil would never be able to set a single hoof anywhere near, to harm them again.

'And this is what the young preacher set about doing. He locked himself in the chapel, wouldn't accept food or water, just knelt at the foot of the altar and prayed hour after hour, day and night. The farmers tried to get him to eat, to at least take some sustenance, but he wouldn't stop in his devotion for even one minute, because he knew how close the devil was. He could feel him breathing down his young neck, needling at his heart and resolve. And the devil soon realised he had a real battle on his hands.

'So he brought Hell with him to that hillside, and crashed it down on the little chapel. He sent apparitions to the young preacher; demons with bats' wings and heads of dogs to bite and maul him. But the young man prayed on. So the devil raised the ghosts of witches who'd been burned at the stake, their hair still blazing, their flesh still cooking. They tried to tempt the preacher, changing their looks to those of beautiful young women, soft to the touch, seducing him with words and naked bodies. But the preacher still refused to give in and run, so they tore at his body with their burning hands. And the young man fought them back with his prayers, whatever they tried to do to him.

'And the devil was weakening now. Four days and four nights the preacher had been keeping him at bay. He could feel his power and his hold over the chapel and the farmers loosening. He was losing his hold, and the battle. He realised how strong in his faith this preacher was, and knew that he had to be clever to beat him. He had to make him suffer in ways only the preacher himself would understand. So he sent an army of spirits across the land to find out where this young preacher had come from, to search for a way to pierce his heart and shatter his faith.

'The devil had to wait another two days and two nights before his minions returned to him, but they brought him the knowledge he craved. It seemed the young man had become a preacher after his family had been murdered by robbers who'd attacked them on the road from London. And the devil raised the bodies of the young man's dead family one by one, to visit him.

'He didn't try to hide what either the bandits or two years of death had done to the bodies, but let them appear as they came straight from the ground. The father came in the morning, with the gaping knife wounds in his neck and chest. The mother came in the afternoon to greet her son. Her skull was battered, crushed, and she spoke in broken words as her teeth rattled inside her head. But the preacher somehow held on to his resolve, somehow was able to see through the devil's illusions.

'Of course these were only the empty bodies of his family, made to move like puppets by the devil; their souls were up in Heaven, and the young preacher kept on telling himself this over and over. But in the evening his sister came to him. The robbers had broken her legs to stop her from running away and then they had beaten and raped her. When she appeared to her brother she had to use her arms to drag herself across the ground, her twisted-up legs trailing through the dirt behind her as she called out to him. And the preacher couldn't take any more, his will was suddenly broken. He could no longer fight, so he ran away. He ran from the chapel screaming, half-mad, half-blind from the horrors he'd seen. He leaped astride his unsaddled horse and galloped away into the hills.

'The devil chased him. The devil wanted him dead, not just gone. He realised how strong the young preacher could be if given time to recover his wits.

He hunted him down, pursuing him across the downs and fells, driving him out of the caves and gullies where he was trying to hide. And the young man ran for his life.

'Eventually he came across a valley. It was a very narrow valley, like a crack in the earth, and he suddenly remembered his teachings about the devil. Not the Bible teachings from Sunday school, but the tales his mother had told him as a child. He remembered her telling him that the devil couldn't jump. She'd said that angels had wings so they could fly above the devil's head, and if he could jump he could catch hold of one and make it carry him back up to Heaven. So God had given him hooves instead of feet, which made it impossible for him to jump. He remembered his mother's words and knew that if he could get across to the other side of the narrow valley, he would be safe because the devil wouldn't be able to follow him.

'The devil was very close, gaining on him with every second. He was almost upon him when the preacher dug his heels into his horse's sides and galloped towards the edge of the narrow, jagged valley. He raced his horse as fast as he could, as fast as the beast would go, and tried to leap across from one side to the other. The devil almost had hold of its tail, was spitting curses at the preacher because he knew what the man was trying to do.

'But either the valley was too wide, or the horse too tired. Or maybe even the devil had gotten a hold of its tail and held it back. Because both the young preacher and his dark, chestnut horse fell to their death. They nearly made it; people say that some of the marks in the rocks are caused by the horse's hooves, where they scrabbled for purchase on the far side. But they fell to the bottom of the valley, crashing against the rocks. It was one battle the devil won.

'Well, almost. He killed the young preacher all right, but the man had already laid enough blessings on the chapel and the farmers, so the devil could do little more than inflict bad luck on the two families. Which is, of course, what he immediately set about doing. But the farmers had survived so much already that they knew they could struggle with a little bad luck. And soon the devil got bored with losing shoes or carrying pebbles on the wind to crack windows, and moved on to other crimes elsewhere.

'One of the farms has gone now, but the chapel

still stands, I've seen it. It stands on the hillside and still has the cobbled pathway leading up to its door and the carved angels to greet you as soon as you step inside. But there are no flowers any more. Haven't been for a long time, and the walls are gradually crumbling away. It still attracts visitors, though, but I suppose because it's more of an oddity these days, than anything else. It's no longer cared for or looked after, it's become as ugly and empty as the hills. So as I say, maybe this was one battle the devil won.'

Joseph stared into the fire. The Leap was only a few metres away, behind the shelter of the Lego rocks. He wasn't sure whether he could hear the sound of a horse's whinny, or just a noise carried by the wind.

Chapter Twelve

Don moved towards the tent and poked his head inside. Joseph lay still, pretending to be asleep. 'Out like a light,' his father said and moved quietly away to regain his place by the fire.

Joseph had retreated into the tent and the welcome, cosy warmth of his sleeping bag not long after Tom had finished his story. The old man and his father were still sitting in the flickering glow from the fire talking quietly, their tall, elongated shadows cast against the canvas wall. A few moments ago the old man had produced a bottle of whisky from his pack and its silhouette was passed back and forth between theirs.

'He's done well to keep up today,' Tom said.

Don nodded and took a drink from the bottle.

'We've walked some miles,' Tom continued. 'Most his age would've done nothing but whine, but I can't say I've heard a peep out of him all day.'

Joseph felt a quick thrill of achievement and

approval at the old man's words. He watched the men's shadows, the flutter of the light thrown by the fire making their outlines soft and vague on the side of the tent. It was like watching a magic lantern show.

'Not that I've heard him string more than two words together all weekend, come to think of it.'

Don shook his shadow-head slowly, but it was a gesture of acquiescence. 'I guess things aren't really working out the way I was hoping,' he admitted.

'He certainly seems to have a chip on his shoulder when it comes to you.'

'Don't I know it.' He took another drink and shrugged. 'I can understand if he's got problems. I know it must be hard for him with, well . . . But hey, I'm trying. And he won't even give me an inch, you know?'

The old man was quiet. Joseph watched as Don lifted the shadow-bottle up to his shadow-head again. He squirmed privately. There was a peculiar edge to his father's voice, a trembling, sentimental edge. He had the terrible premonition that Don was going to get drunk and spill his guts to Tom. And Joseph didn't think he could stand that. He didn't think he could stand his father getting all worked-up and emotional.

He'd only seen Don cry once before, and that was when his grandma had died, but it had probably been the most embarrassing moment of his life. He'd had to leave the room.

The silence stretched out between the men. Joseph saw Cos move to sit by his master, and their two shadows merged to make one rather awkward-shaped silhouette. Don took yet another drink, then offered it to Tom with a mumbled apology for keeping it so long.

But Tom wouldn't accept it. 'You look as though you could use it more than me,' he said. And Joseph cringed in his sleeping bag.

'You sure you don't mind hearing this?' Don asked.

Tom shook his head. 'I've run out of stories, anyway,' he said.

Don chuckled sardonically. 'What is this? Jackanory?' He hunched himself over, leaning towards the fire, and his shadow grew that little bit larger on the side of the tent. Joseph squeezed his eyes shut as if it would help block out what was coming next. He tried to think about his *Watership Down* cover, tried to visualise the picture, the colours, the way it looked on his desk in his bedroom.

'We separated, Helen and I, a little over five years ago. I just upped and left, walked out on her and Joe. Poof; vanished; suitcase under my arm and I was gone. And you know what the stupid thing is? The really stupid thing? I honestly don't think I could tell you why. Crazy, eh? I was ready to throw away twelve years of marriage, and looking back I don't even know why.'

Joseph needed to pee. The sensation suddenly gripped him. He thought harder about his cover to stop him thinking about the need. It was two rabbits fighting, a seagull swooping, but it wasn't finished yet. But the cold, tickling, anxious feeling crawled through him, making him roll over on to his stomach and press himself against the hard ground.

'I didn't even have anywhere else to go. That's how crazy it was. I hadn't got anything planned. It wasn't as if I had another woman waiting for me or anything like that. Yeah, we seemed to be arguing a lot, and I admit I was unhappy in my job, unfulfilled, and I guess the sex didn't seem so good any more, not like when we'd been younger. But it wasn't as though there were any major fights with crockery and pieces of furniture flying around. Nothing like that.

Nothing that I suppose any average couple doesn't have to go through as par for the course. But this is all in hindsight. At the time, I . . . Well, I just felt I needed out.' He paused to take on more whisky. 'I don't know. Mid-life crisis at thirty-four. Crazy.'

Joseph cupped himself in his hand and squeezed. He didn't dare move. He couldn't let his father know he was still awake; still listening. But his need to pee was *so* bad. He squeezed hard enough to make it hurt, and the pain temporarily took the edge off his need.

'I didn't go far, I just got myself a little flat on the other side of town. And I kept in touch. I never forgot birthdays, I was always popping round to see Joseph, taking him out places, helping him with his schoolwork, everything. I still wanted an active role in his life, as a father. The only difference was, I didn't live with him any more.

'I never saw much of Helen, admittedly. I guess I just didn't know how to face her, didn't know what to say to her. Looking back, I suppose I was trying to find myself, you know? I'd lost touch with who I really was. Work, marriage; it had all dragged me down. And this is crazy, right?' More whisky. 'But one day, I suddenly realised that I'd never been water-skiing. And, yeah, OK, I know its sounds crazy, but as a kid I'd always had this ambition to go water-skiing. And somehow I'd forgotten all about it. The idea had just been lost over the years. And I began to wonder what else had maybe gotten lost; what other ambitions had I had? What else had I wanted to do with my life? I couldn't think of many, admittedly, but I sure as hell went water-skiing that very next day. I just drove down to this water sports place about thirty-odd miles away and did it there and then. It was great. I loved it. It was everything I'd always dreamed it to be. It was just a pity it didn't last longer. You don't get a lot of time for your money, you see. It's about forty quid for a couple of hours. But I'm going to go back someday. Definitely. I really enjoyed it. It was really great. Superb.'

Joseph was getting cramps in his stomach. He had to go soon. He was desperately trying to hold it off for as long as he could. He squirmed uncomfortably inside his sleeping bag. He wished his father would shut up.

'Anyway, to cut a long story short, the insanity lasted for a full five years. Well, to be honest, the insanity lasted me about three, stubbornness and pride saw me through the final two.'

Tell him about Trudy, Joseph was thinking. Tell Tom how many years her and her Vodafone saw you through.

'We never divorced, you see. We never really talked about it. Maybe I always knew I'd come to my senses eventually. And, you know, things had changed. I'd changed. I'd also made a bit of a career move. I told you about it, remember? I'd been offered this position at a firm of solicitors. Better money, better prospects and everything seemed to slot back into place. Just like that.' He snapped his fingers, shook his head. 'Crazy.' And took another mouthful of whisky.

'So I said to myself, I said, Don, there's just one thing missing now, old lad. And you know what that is, don't you? It's your family. It's the people who love you most. You see, the new job, it'd given me the new start I'd been looking for. Fresh hope, you see? And I knew Helen'd take me back. I knew she'd be waiting for me.'

Joseph had to go. Right now. He was going to pee in his sleeping bag if he didn't get up and go right this very second. So he made as much noise as possible, shuffling around noisily, unzipping the bag when really there was no need, and fumbling his way out of the tent. The cold hit him as he stepped into the open, instantly making him shiver. The two men turned to look at him, but he avoided their eyes and walked quickly round the other side of the tent. The grass was freezing between his toes. He saw his father take another drink from the bottle. He went to pee up against the rocks, but had to wait for what seemed like an age for anything to happen.

'I thought he would've been happy,' his father said in a hushed voice that clearly was not hushed enough. 'I would've thought any kid'd be happy to get their dad back, you know? Yeah, maybe if I'd never gone back. But I'd made a mistake. I've admitted it, right?' He shook his head. 'I don't know if it's me or what.'

That same old burning resentment rose in Joseph again. He finished, but stood for a few seconds gritting his teeth against it. Only when he felt in control of it did he return to the tent.

Don had been watching him all the time. At least Tom had been gracious enough to keep his back turned.

'Hey, Joe. Hey,' his father called, his voice thick and furry. 'Come sit with us, Joe. It's a beautiful night. Nice an' warm by the fire.'

But Joseph ignored him. He crawled deep down into the sleeping bag and pulled it high up over his head, curling himself into a tight ball to try and get warm again. His feet were like blocks of ice.

'See what I mean? I can't do anything for him. He just shuts me out every time. This weekend, it was supposed to, you know . . . An' then when we met you, an' there was this hunting thing, an' I thought, Hey. I thought, That's gonna be better than any fishing trip, right? You know, something to tell his mates about back at school. Going on a hunting trip with the old man. You see it all the time in the movies, yeah?'

'Five years is a long time,' Tom put in. The first thing he'd said since Don had started talking. 'Especially at that age. He's probably done a lot of growing up. Had to, no doubt.'

'He's still just a kid though,' Don said. He sounded angry. 'God, Tom, he's only fifteen, right? He still needs a father.'

Tom didn't answer.

*

Joseph was woken during the night. He had no idea what time it was; it was pitch-black and he couldn't see his watch. He could hear his father puking somewhere in the darkness outside.

Chapter Thirteen

There had been a gossamer mist lying low on the ground when Joseph had woken this morning, and it had seeped into him, chilling his bones. It had taken all of his willpower to climb out of the snug sleeping bag, but he had done it because he'd remembered Tom's words of approval last night. The old man and his dog were already up and about, impatient to get going, making Joseph wonder if they had, in fact, slept at all.

'Breakfast?' the old man asked. The boy nodded, and Tom handed him a chicken leg left over from the night before, and a chunk of pork-pie. Joseph had never really liked pork-pies, but he ate it anyway, knowing the old man was watching him.

Tom didn't take his eyes off the boy. He was crouched beside the dead fire, his dog sitting on the wet grass next to him. He scratched between the old collie's ears. 'Times like this I could really use a cigarette,' he said. 'First one of the day is the one I miss most.'

Joseph nodded as if he understood, feeling awkward in the old man's gaze. Eating the pork-pie made him realise how hungry he was, and he quickly started on the chicken leg.

'Your father's had to go to the toilet,' Tom said, and nodded behind himself, in the general direction of behind the rocks. 'He shouldn't be too long.' He was watching Joseph so closely that the boy felt as if he expected some sort of reply.

So he swallowed his mouthful of chicken and asked, 'Do you think we'll find it today? The cat, I mean.'

'If it's down there.'

Joseph nodded again, but didn't look up at the man. 'Do you think it's like Mr Hooper said it is?' he asked carefully.

'A devil?' The old man laughed. 'I don't believe in Art Hooper's devils any more than I believe your father telling me it's from out of space.'

'When did he say it was from outer space?' Joseph couldn't remember that bit, but it sounded pathetic enough to be something his father *would* say.

'He tried to tell me it was a Martian. Or was "alien" the word he used?'

'Oh, no, I don't think he meant it like that,' Joseph said. 'I think he meant alien as in "not natural" or "foreign". It's just a name scientists use . . .' He saw the way Tom was watching him and added, 'I think.' Then took another bite of his cold chicken leg, even though his appetite had suddenly evaporated.

'You don't get on with your father, do you?'

Joseph didn't answer. He watched the chicken leg as he turned it over in his fingers.

'I suppose I can understand that,' Tom said, 'but I want you to know, he's not a bad man, Joseph. He may very well be selfish, and can more often than not be stupid too, by the looks of him, but I really don't think he's hurting you on purpose.'

'You don't know him,' Joseph mumbled, angry that Tom was taking his father's side.

'No,' the old man agreed. 'No, I don't know him, I've only just met him. But I think I've more than likely *been* him. Why d'you think my son's living all the way down in London, and I'm up here by myself?' He patted Cos on the head. 'And see the lad here? Why d'you think he was named like he was? And why d'you think you've never heard me call him by it?'

'It's not the same.'

Tom shrugged. 'Mebbe not quite, but . . .'

'He tries to rule my life. He's come back and he's always telling me what to do. I'm not ten any more. He's still treating me as if I'm a little kid or something.'

'So tell him,' the old man said gently. 'He'll not understand unless you tell him.'

'He'll never understand,' Joseph said bitterly.

'You may be surprised what . . .'

'I hate him. I wish he was dead.'

Tom shook his head. 'Childish words like that won't do you any good, sonny.'

Joseph knew it was childish, but everything his father had said last night came flooding back to him; all the proof he needed to show how little the man understood his feelings. He stood up and angrily threw the half-eaten chicken leg into the grey ashes of the cold fire.

'I hope we find the cat and it kills him.'

Chapter Fourteen

They stood on the edge of The Leap and looked down.

It was a narrow valley with craggy rock walls. It was a jagged crack in the hills, struck open by a thunderbolt or torn apart by the claws of a giant. A few sparse trees clung to the steep sides, their thick roots like talons gripping the loose soil. A thin, twisting, vein-like river ran along the bottom. Clumps of gorse and tangled bushes hugged the water's edge. The valley was maybe only two hundred metres across at its widest point, but it was a tear in the countryside running into the distance for as far as the eye could see.

Down into The Leap. The soil was loose underneath their feet, crumbling away into miniature avalanches. Don slipped twice on to his backside, his new rucksack breaking his fall. They had to pick their way between the rocks, choosing which ones looked safe enough to hang on to. Even Cos had problems. His two front legs were splayed in front of him, his head held low as he half-slid, half-staggered his way down into the valley. But he made it to the bottom first, and then waited for the others to catch up. Joseph planted his feet carefully, he clung to one tree then another, using them to slow his headlong progress.

'It's not much like I remember it to be,' Don said when he finally joined Cos, Tom and Joseph at the bottom. The sides of the valley rose high on either side. Massive boulders that had rolled or slipped down the rock-face maybe as long as a thousand years ago lay all around. They began walking, following the flow of the tumbling river. Grass was trying to grow close to the water's edge – green grass, proper grass – but had only managed to succeed in patches. The water itself was clear, in some places you could see the pebbles that lined the bottom, but it was a fast and furious little stream, frothing and spitting against the chunks of rock that disturbed its flow.

'This isn't where you would've come fishing,' Tom told him. 'The river broadens out further down. You would have come in by the old road, not the way we walked, and there's a shack where the fishermen can stay the night. The river pools up close to it; looks almost like a little lake.'

Don nodded. 'I remember that shack,' he said. 'There're several little cots or beds inside, aren't there? No sheets or anything. I can remember this old boy asleep on one of them still wearing his waders, cuddling his rod and resting his head on his bait box. I wanted to go inside and have a look around but my dad wouldn't let me.' He grinned at the memory.

'Aye, that's the place,' Tom said.

'Is it far from here?'

'Not too far. It's where we'll be spending the night.'

'Is it still standing? God, it was on its last legs when I was there all those years ago, it must be a bit of a sorry sight nowadays.'

'It'll save messing with a tent,' Tom told him. 'Safer, too.'

They walked in a southerly direction; the sun on Joseph's left would rise, cross over his head and set on his right. Occasionally they had to clamber over the fallen boulders that blocked their path, and at one point they were forced to cross over the stream. Joseph walked behind the two men, wishing all the more that he wasn't here, now. Tom hadn't spoken to him since his little outburst and he felt somehow chastised, as if he'd been returned back into the old man's school for whiny little kids. Not that he regretted what he'd said, but he wanted to talk to Tom again, only this time try to explain things better.

Tom however, didn't seem to be in the frame of mind for talking any more. Don was busy reliving his childhood fishing trip and all the old man had to offer was the occasional grunt. He seemed to be becoming more withdrawn by the minute. Joseph remembered how he'd given off a certain air of hostility when they'd first met him, and now sensed the same air of aggression growing within the man the further they walked, the longer the morning wore on. Or maybe it was the closer they got.

The canvas bag had been discarded and now Tom carried his gun broken open over his arm, like the poacher in the picture at The Retreat. Joseph would have liked to ask if he could take a look at the gun, but he knew his father wouldn't let him, even if Tom would. He'd drawn dozens of guns for his covers, but he'd never actually seen one in real life before, he'd only ever copied them from pictures in magazines. And he'd never drawn this type of gun before. It was a double-barrelled shotgun, a reflective black that caught the sunlight. Only it kind of glistened, it didn't shine. It looked very thick, very heavy, solid. With it being broken open across the old man's arm Joseph could see the two brass caps of the shells, each inside their separate barrel.

Even Don wasn't as sprightly this morning as he had been. His childhood memories soon dried up and he simply plodded along beside Tom. He may not have said as much but Joseph guessed his second hangover in as many mornings had taken its toll on him. His unshaven Flintstone Face looked dirty and tired, and he seemed to be struggling a little with his new rucksack. He walked with his hands holding on to the shoulder straps as if they were braces, and kept trying to hitch it higher up his back. Its nice new colours were scuffed and grazed with mud. He had tried to talk to Joseph, but the boy had made it plain he wasn't interested in talking back. The fact that Don had given up on him more easily than usual only went to prove how under the weather he must be feeling this morning.

Joseph followed the two men, who followed the dog. And once again his thoughts returned to his one and only conversation with Tom. He watched the two men in front of him. He thought about what Tom had said, about how maybe he should talk to his father, make him listen, stand up to him and force him to understand. And Joseph suddenly realised that the old man had been right all along, he really was very similar to Don. After all, it had been the only time he'd actually bothered to talk to Joseph, and all he'd done was to tell him how to run his life. So yes, Joseph thought, that sounded very much like his father. In fact, that was exactly the sort of thing his father would do. Not that he should have expected anything else of course, adults were bound to stick up for each other, they always did. But it still hurt; he felt cheated. He'd thought Tom was different.

That age-old and familiar resentment heated the boy's belly against the wind. It was easy to find the sour mood that had always been its companion and he soon folded himself down into it.

He just wanted to go home now. He just wanted to get out of these hills and back into the warmth and solitude of his bedroom, with the new cover he was working on. Of course, he knew it would do no good to tell his father as much, no matter how much he stood up to him. So he'd just have to shut up and go along with it all like a good little boy. He shivered in the wind and looked about himself at the forbidding valley walls. Then at the two men playing at safari up ahead of him. They were certainly a sorry sight for big game hunters everywhere. What were they doing here? And even if it actually did exist, how on earth did they expect to find this cat? Paw prints? Trails of blood? Dung heaps full of sheep brains? Or would the cat leap out at them, shout, Here I am, shoot me now! and let Tom blow it away?

In fact, the boy was so deep inside his sullen mood that he didn't even notice Cos when he started barking, and Don had to grab his arm.

The old collie had a gruff, chuffing kind of bark that showed his age, but it also showed his teeth. His tail was down between his legs. He snapped and snarled nastily.

'What is it, lad? What've you found?' Tom took a step towards his dog. 'I think he's picked up a scent,' he called over his shoulder.

'Stay back,' Don told Joseph.

Cos growled threateningly. He took a step forwards, his lips curled back over his teeth.

'Steady there, lad.'

'What can you see?' Don asked. But didn't get any closer. 'Do you think . . .'

Tom snapped the shotgun closed as he walked over to the old collie. The two shiny, brass caps of the shells disappeared within the gun's heavy black.

Joseph wanted to go too, but Don held him back.

Cos's barks echoed off The Leap's high rock walls.

'Good lad. Steady now.' Tom patted the old collie's back.

'What can you see?' Don repeated.

Tom lifted the gun in both hands. Tumbled rocks as big as cars were half hidden by a tangle of bushes and trees close to the base of the valley's wall. He stepped slowly and carefully towards the mass of undergrowth. He followed the dog's barks, peering into the bushes, his eyes trying to pierce the heavy foliage. Then he looked at the ground. He stopped and knelt slowly.

'There's tracks,' he said.

Chapter Fifteen

'Joe. Get your camera. Quick, now.'

Joseph felt the sudden need to giggle as his nerves kicked in. He bit his lip. But then something cold crawled in his belly, killing the sensation dead.

His father shrugged his new rucksack off his shoulders in such a hurry that he didn't even bother to see where it fell. 'Come on, Joseph. Quickly.'

Joseph took his own rucksack off his back and handed it to his father, who was then too busy digging around inside the pockets to hold him back any more. So he walked over to where Tom was standing, not at all sure what he was expecting to see. It was still all a game, right? Had to be, didn't it?

Tom glanced over his shoulder at him as the boy approached, standing back up again but using the shotgun to point down at the mud.

And there they were.

Undeniable.

Joseph felt disbelief roll over him in a wave,

leaving him dizzy, leaving him icy and nauseous. They were clear in the soft mud, paw prints, twice the size of Cos's next to them; padded impressions in the dirt, leading up to the bushes. The wind moved through the leaves, gently shushing them against each other.

'Are they definitely a cat's?' he asked, almost whispering.

'Can't see what else they could be,' the old man said. 'Can you?' The hostile air that had been growing around him was dense now. He took his shotgun in both hands again as if testing its weight, never taking his eyes from the bushes, and breathed hard through his nose.

Cos growled quietly and the noise rippled along his whole length. He held his tail down.

Don had found the camera. 'Come away, Joseph. Come back from there.'

'Better do as your father says.'

The boy moved back slowly. He took a breath, and held it as a second wave of disbelief washed over him. It suddenly wasn't a game any more. The cat existed; Tom really meant to kill it. He wanted to look at the prints again, just to make sure. But his father had grabbed his arm and pulled him away. He crouched down to ease the queasiness in his stomach. He'd told Tom that he believed in the cat, but he knew now that he hadn't, not really, not until now. He tried to understand what the cat being real meant to him, but wasn't quite able to. His head was spinning. He'd been so sure it was make-believe. For all its ridiculousness, for all its absurdity . . .

Tom walked towards the high bushes, Cos at his heel. The leaves were yellowing, going brown; he used the gun to push them aside. Don had let go of Joseph and held the boy's camera with both hands out in front of him, but he seemed to have forgotten he had hold of it at all. The river's rushing water was noisy behind them. Tom stepped into the bushes and the branches and leaves closed all too easily around him, almost like water themselves, stealing him from view. Joseph watched in silence, waited, still crouching.

'There's bones,' Tom suddenly shouted, making the boy jump. 'Rabbits, I think. Two or three of them, by the looks of it.'

Neither Joseph – nor his father made a move.

'It's definitely been here,' Tom called. 'But I think we've missed it.'

Don moved hesitantly towards the bushes himself

now. He turned to Joseph. 'Are you coming to see?'

The boy nodded slowly and got to his feet again. He followed his father through the tangled branches of the tall bushes.

There was a peculiar smell to the air inside the bushes; not quite sweat, it reminded Joseph of damp, dirty clothes. The bushes and trees crowded around to enclose them in a kind of hollow, with the sunlight struggling to pierce the tight, net-like cover of the foliage. The massive rocks stood on the far side, all pitted and scarred. Tom was standing in the centre, the rabbit bones lay scattered all around him. They were pale and white, jagged and splintered at the ends.

'It's definitely been here,' he repeated, nodding, and Don took a photograph of the bones.

Cos was still growling, his body still tense. He started barking again. He snapped and snarled at the base of the massive rocks. Don grabbed Joseph's arm, once more pulling him back and away. There was a gap, an angular hole between two of the boulders, where one rested against the other. Tom got down on his haunches to see. The darkness in the hole led away and back underneath the rocks. It looked just about big enough for a man to squeeze inside.

'Steady, lad. Steady.'

Slowly, carefully, Tom edged his way towards the hole. He moved his head from side to side, trying to see into the darkness. He patted the old collie's back and waved for the dog to give him room. Again he moved that tiny pace closer. Then clicked his fingers at Cos to shoo him to one side. And this time the dog reluctantly obeyed. He growled threateningly at the hole, baring his yellow, pointed teeth, but moved all the same.

Don began, 'Tom, maybe you shouldn't . . .' But he didn't finish.

The pit of Joseph's stomach was hollow. The grip his father had on his arm was painful. He realised that the smell inside the bushes was of wet fur.

The old man ducked his head and squinted into the hole, but it was too dark to see more than a few inches. He held his gun out in front of him. He gently tapped the black barrel against the rough edge of the boulder, the metal scraping on the rock. Cos barked and the old man shushed him. He lowered himself carefully on to his belly. Again Cos barked.

'Quiet!'

He wriggled forwards and rapped the barrels of

the shotgun sharply against the rock. Nothing happened. He waited. He did it one more time; a dull, clanging sound. Cos skittered over his legs from one side of the gap to the other. Then back again. He could *almost* have looked excited. Tom squeezed himself into the hole.

His head, then his shoulders disappeared into the darkness. He crawled on his belly until only his backside and his legs were visible. It looked like the hole was eating him up. Cos was running from one side of the gap to the other, whimpering, whining, back and forth. He tried to dig his way into the hole with his master. His claws scratched anxiously at the rock.

'Tom, I really think . . .'

Joseph heard a low, hissing growl coming from the hole and his father instantly shut up. Cos started barking, started frantically biting at the rock. Tom cried out, his legs kicking. Don made to run forwards. And the shotgun boomed.

Tom was screaming. Cos was barking. The valley shook with the noise of the gun. Don was shouting, 'Tom! Tom!' The ground quaked beneath Joseph's feet. He was tipped on to his backside. Tom's legs kicked the ground. Trying to find purchase, trying to pull himself free of the hole. Cos was wild. Joseph was frozen. Don grabbed Tom's leg. Plucked him from between the rocks. He . . . Joseph saw the blood. Tom was trying to stand. Spilling from him. Cos was in the hole. Don's hands were in the air. Streaks of red on the man's bald head. Don was panicked, warding him off. There was so much blood. Cos snapped at the darkness in the hole. 'God, Tom.' Streaks of red on the bald man's skull. 'Oh, God!' Tom couldn't see for blood. Don couldn't see for blood; staggering backwards, away. Tom couldn't stand. Claw marks. Cos yelped. There were claw marks on Tom's bald head. Tom slumped forward on to his knees. Cos was bloody too. And it came from the darkness of the hole.

It was huge; as long as a man is tall. Pale like a ghost it leaped from its den, tumbling the old collie to one side, hissing and spitting like the demon Art Hooper claimed it to be. Its face was twisted and savage, purely feral, its ears flat to its head. Its teeth and claws were already bloody. Joseph saw it leap at Tom

Beverly and he tried to cry out, he tried to shout. But the teeth had already bitten down, cracking, splitting and tearing. The old man squealed like a baby. He was slammed forwards, his body raising dust as it hit the ground. The shotgun went off in his hand, booming, kicking itself free of his grip.

The noise shook the air, the trees, the earth on which Joseph had fallen. Don cried out. Joseph thought it was at the sight of the cat, but there was a bright explosion like a burst of red rose petals from his shoulder and his father was punched backwards and twisted through the air. His feet were lifted all the way off the ground.

The cat spat its hatred at Joseph. It hissed at him, with blazing eyes. It could have had him, it could have killed him in an instant, right there and then. And there would have been nothing in the world he could have done to stop it. But the cat turned, its lithe body curling to spring itself forwards in a loping run and it crashed away through the bushes.

Cos gave chase, yapping and barking. Joseph simply sat still and quiet and waited for the trembling in the ground to subside. Then he started to weep.

Chapter Sixteen

'Joseph? Joseph, can you hear me?'

Tom Beverly was face-down in the dirt. He lay still.

'Joseph? Joe?'

The boy wanted to go over and nudge him, kick him, force him to move. He wanted the old man to leap to his feet and shout, Surprise! But Joseph didn't move, and neither did the old man.

The tears came again. Huge tears that choked him and hurt his chest as they were dredged up from the very bottom of his soul. His world had been pulled inside out. He felt as if it had all been ripped apart and left torn and ragged around the edges. He was shivering. He knew he needed to stand and walk away, it was just that he wasn't able to move just yet. The quaking of the valley after the noise of the gun had settled in his limbs.

'Joseph, please . . .'

He turned to look at his father. The man was sprawled awkwardly on his back, his chest heaving with each breath, a dark patch spreading from the big, black hole in his shoulder. He tried to sit up, but couldn't manage it. He screwed his eyes tight shut for two, maybe three seconds, then stared back up into the canopy of leaves above him. The sunlight was weak on his thin face, making his skin seem almost transparent. He struggled with his words.

'My phone, Joe. Get my phone.'

Joseph had an autopilot. He'd never known about it before, had probably never needed to use it before, but it slowly came to life now. Because it pushed him up on to his shaky feet, and then pushed him back through the bushes and down to the river, to where Don had dropped his rucksack. It was like being the star of a movie. He felt as though he was watching himself through the camera, looking at his body wandering about of its own accord. He started with a wide-angled shot, then drew in for a close-up of the expression on his face, and wasn't at all surprised to see how blank he looked. He saw himself walk past his own rucksack, looking around for the one with the bright colours. He even seemed to notice it sitting in the water before his body did. So he pointed it out to himself.

His father had been too excited about getting a photo of the cat to worry about where he'd dropped his new rucksack, and he'd been standing right at the water's edge. It must have bounced and rolled behind him into the stream. Luckily the river hadn't carried it too far, and being the size it was it had wedged itself behind one of the many rocks jutting up to break the water's surface. Even in Joseph's disjointed state of mind he realised that if the phone was wet it wouldn't work, and he felt peculiarly fearful about wading into the river to retrieve it. But he couldn't quite figure out why.

Because if he got hold of the phone then he could call the police, or his mother, even Trevor Toomey to come and pick them up in his taxi. The phone could be their saviour. They were lost in the hills, miles from anywhere, his father badly injured. That little mobile phone could save their lives.

But that was only if it still worked.

He still stood on the bank, not quite willing to move, overriding his autopilot. He watched the bright rucksack as it bobbed up and down. It gently bumped into the rock that blocked its path, the water spitting and frothing all around it.

Slowly he took his boots off. Then his socks, then his jeans. He stepped into the icy water and waded out towards the rucksack, never taking his eyes from it. The river rose past his knees, rose to his waist, splashing up around him as high as his chest. The sharp stones and hard pebbles on the river's bed hurt his feet. He tried to hold his breath against the cold. He grabbed the rucksack's colourful straps and dragged it to him, then held it above his head as he waded back to the bank. He didn't even wait to dry himself off before he pulled on the toggles to open the rucksack up. He pulled jumpers and pants out, all sodden, tossing them aside. He tipped the rucksack upside down and the bundle of a sleeping bag and trousers fell out, the phone with them. Joseph snatched it up only to see damp misting in the corners of the tiny display. He ignored it. He pressed the buttons, he pulled the aerial up, but the little phone wouldn't show any signs of life. He tipped it upside down to see if the battery was clipped on properly. And water trickled out of the mouthpiece.

He stood and shivered, his autopilot feeling all used up.

And he may very well have stood there like that

for ever if he hadn't seen Cos coming back along the bottom of the valley. Seeing the old collie kicked his head back into gear, he called out to it. The dog trotted towards him, but then went to the bushes and pushed its way through them back into the little hollow. Joseph pulled his soaking underpants off and quickly dressed again without them. He followed the way Cos had gone through the bushes.

There was a different smell in the hollow now; thick, but sweet. Tom was still twisted and torn, face down on the ground. It came as a shock to the boy that he was still dead, he'd almost forgotten about what had happened. And even looking at the body, the gore still leaking out of it, Joseph felt somehow disconnected from everything that had gone on. It was a feeling something similar to déjà vu. He couldn't quite work out if it had all actually happened or not. Or if he'd maybe only imagined certain parts, here and there.

The dog sniffed its master's corpse carefully, walking all the way around the tattered body. Then sat itself down on the ground next to it. Joseph called the dog to him, but Cos didn't move. Joseph walked over to the old collie, keeping his eyes on the dog and off Tom. It had blood on its muzzle from the wound across its nose. He took hold of the dog's collar.

'Come on, Cos. Come on now.'

The old collie refused to move. So Joseph pulled harder, started to physically drag the dog away. 'Come on, lad,' Joseph said. 'You can't stay here.'

But the dog bared its teeth, growling threateningly. It wasn't going to be taken from its master's side, and reluctantly Joseph had to let go of it.

'The phone, Joe. Did you get the phone?'

He was startled by the sound of his father's voice. He'd forgotten about him, as well.

Don had managed to sit up slightly and was leaning back on the trunk of a tree. For all his dirty stubble, his face was so very pale. He had blood encrusted in his chin-button.

'It's broken.'

'What do you mean? It can't be.'

'You dropped your rucksack in the river. Everything's soaked.'

'It should still work.'

'It won't. I tried . . .'

'Let me see. It's got to be working.'

'I think the water got behind the battery.'

'Let me see. We've got to call someone.'

'I tried all the buttons and . . .'

'Fetch me it, Joseph! I want to see for myself!' His chest heaved with his breath and he squeezed his eyes closed against the pain. 'It's got to work.'

Joseph brought the little phone to him. He crouched down next to his father. 'There's damp on the screen, you see. And the buttons . . .'

'Give it to me!'

Joseph handed it to him and watched as he went through the same routine Joseph had gone through earlier. Then watched him go through it again.

'See, it's . . .'

'Shut up!' Don unclipped the battery, awkwardly because he was only able to use one hand. He rubbed it on his trousers, trying to dry some of the water, then clipped it back on again, and went through the button-pressing one more time. He swore and threw the phone at the rocks. It cracked loudly against them and Cos growled menacingly at him.

Don's chest heaved and fell, heaved and fell. Joseph thought he looked as though his autopilot was now fading on him too. The wound in his shoulder wasn't as clean as it had appeared at first, but was dozens of tiny, bloody tears in his cagoule, across the flat of his shoulder where the shot had hit him. Only a few inches lower and it would have hit his heart. Someone could have smeared the blood on with a thick paintbrush, it was a crusty black in some places, sticky and glistening in others.

'We'll have to go back to that old man's house,' Don said. 'Cooper, or whatever the hell he was called. I know he hasn't got a phone, but he must have some kind of contact with the outside world.'

Joseph nodded. He helped his father to stand, the man hissing at the pain.

'You'd better get the gun,' Don told him. He leaned himself up against a tree and nodded at the shotgun, lying just out of Tom Beverly's dead reach. 'I don't want to be without it if that cat comes back.' His words were harsh, but his voice was weary.

Joseph did as he was told, Cos growling at him when the dog thought the boy was getting too close to its master's body. Joseph grabbed the shotgun's barrel and pulled it away over the ground. He remembered wanting to see it, wanting to hold it earlier. And now when he picked it up it was as heavy and as solid as he'd expected, but he took no pleasure in the fact.

He helped his father push through the bushes and back out into the open valley. They both saw the steep rock walls together, and both knew that Don was never going to be able to climb them in his state, so there was no way they could retrace their steps back to Art Hooper's. They stood in silence, options slipping away one by one, the wind growing stronger, colder, whipping up the surface of the narrow river. Heavy, grey clouds were gathering overhead. They were going to need some shelter from the oncoming night. They were going to need somewhere away from the cat.

'What about that fishermen's shack you and Tom were talking about?' Joseph asked.

Don turned and looked away down the valley. 'I don't know how far it is,' he said.

'Tom said it wasn't far.'

Don nodded. He winced at the terrible, burning pain in his shoulder. He moved to lean himself back up against a rock and put his hand up to his wound, as if trying to hold the hurt in.

'I guess it's all we can do.' He looked down the valley again. He took a deep, shuddering breath. Then turned to his son.

'I just don't know if I can make it,' he said. And began to cry.

Chapter Seventeen

They stood slightly apart, there was a few feet of stony ground between them, but neither was a hero so they stood and cried together.

And this time Joseph wasn't crying for himself. He didn't need reminding of what he'd said to Tom Beverly earlier that day, but now it was Tom laid face-down in the dirt, and dead. He felt as if maybe his words had been a curse, as if maybe he'd been the cause of Tom's death, and the coming inevitability of his father's. For his father was close, they both knew that. And that was why they stood together and cried.

It was Don who got them moving. Tom still had some food in his pack which they took, and Joseph stuffed his pockets with shells for the shotgun. Everything in Don's rucksack was drenched and cold and so left behind on the riverbank; whatever Joseph carried in his would have to do. He ripped up a T-shirt and tied a makeshift bandage over his father's wound. They both seemed to realise it was purely superficial, but neither of them mentioned it to the other. They tried to call Cos to them, a small hope that the dog would lead them in the right direction, but the old collie still refused to leave its muster's side. And Joseph didn't know whether to admire the dog for its loyalty, or hate it for abandoning them, for leaving them completely alone.

They walked slowly. Don struggled, needing help over the rocky ground. They had to find the long way around a lot of the large, tumbled boulders because he was unable to climb over them. They walked in silence because he had no real breath for conversation. He hung on to Joseph's rucksack, pulling painfully as the straps dug into the boy's shoulders. A dark rose blossomed and grew on the makeshift bandage over his wound. The further they walked, the weaker he became.

The valley twisted and turned. Joseph watched the river, remembering Tom saying that it broadened out before it reached the shack, and maybe it did round this coming bend. Then maybe the next. He couldn't tell how far they'd walked; The Leap led them on and on. Spots of rain were carried in the wind. Every time his father stumbled he thought his own legs were going to shatter beneath him as he fought to support the man's weight. His mind kept on returning to his conversation with Tom. He listened to his father's short breaths.

He thought he saw Cos. But it must have been his imagination. He thought he saw a shape move between the rocks on the opposite side of the river and called out the old collie's name. Although it could have been just a shadow, maybe cast by the clouds as they gathered and grew overhead. He still waited, though. He watched where he thought he'd seen it. He was sure he'd seen something.

The spots of rain got fatter, heavier; the river more ragged, faster flowing. Don's eyes were half closed now. Joseph tried to talk to him, but he didn't seem to hear. He walked as though he was falling forwards on each and every step. The makeshift bandage was sodden and red. The slash of sky above the valley was dark with clouds, growing darker as the night drew closer. They walked with the flow of the river, but it was beating them to every bend, every turn in the winding, twisting valley.

But Joseph realised they were being forced to walk closer to the valley's walls, being pushed further into the rocks by the river as it broadened out. His already exhausted legs pushed him on. There was a sharp turn in the valley up ahead of him. The shack had to be round it. Had to be. Because if it wasn't he knew he wouldn't be able to carry on, he simply wouldn't be able to walk any further. Not with his father. But he pushed that thought aside. He held his head down against the spitting rain and cold, cold wind, watching his feet.

And it *was* there. Broken, hanging over the edge of the bloated river, but it was standing there against the wind and the rain that blew angrily about it. The relief he felt was almost a shelter in itself. He dragged his father towards it, almost finding the strength to run.

The door batted back and forth in the wind, he held it open and hauled his father inside. It was a single room with maybe as many as a dozen bare cots round the edge, a table standing in the middle but no chairs. He let his father slump down on the nearest cot. The shack's walls had been made of slatted wood and there were gaps with several of the slats missing. There was a single grimy window and the glass was cracked.

He took his rucksack off his tender shoulders and pulled his sleeping bag out, unzipping it and laying it over his father. The man's eyes had closed but still showed movement behind the thin lids. He wanted to sleep himself now, he could feel his exhaustion creeping around inside his head. There was a rusty bolt on the inside of the door frame that he had to fight with, but once he'd managed to slide it home it held the door. He turned some of the cots on to their sides and pushed them up against the walls to block the wind as it whistled through the missing slats. He pulled his two spare jumpers on over his coat. He placed the shotgun on the floor at the side of the cot, then finally lay down next to his father on the hard wood. But he wasn't able to sleep.

He listened to the wind and the rain rattle the door, and to Don's laboured breath. He knew his father wasn't going to be able to walk any further. He'd have to go for help alone; leave his father here and try to find his way through the hills and back to Becksall to fetch help. It was their only chance. His father needed a doctor quickly if he had any hope of surviving.

And again Joseph's mind returned to his conversation with Tom.

Chapter Eighteen

He shuddered awake. Night had fallen and the darkness was complete. The wind howled through the shack, he was cold. He held his breath and could hear his father breathing softly but raggedly. The door rattled and banged against itself, the rain pelted down on the wooden roof. But there was something else, beneath it all there was another sound.

He strained his ears, not daring to move.

Someone was out there. He could hear someone moving around outside the shack, their footsteps careful on the small pebbles and sharp stones that littered the ground. He didn't know who, but he knew enough not to call out.

He reached down to the floor at the side of the cot and took hold of the shotgun. Only when he had it held to him did he realise it wasn't loaded, and that he didn't know how to do it.

He fumbled in the dark with clumsy fingers, searching for some sort of catch or button that would break the gun open. Fear was needling at him, he kept losing the sound of the footsteps behind the noise of the wind. He was frightened that whoever was outside could see him through the grimy window, but he couldn't see them. His fingers ran blind across the cold metal. He found a catch. He pushed it with his thumb, he pressed it down, he tried to pluck at it with his fingers, and really didn't know how he'd done it when the gun suddenly broke in two with a loud snapping sound. He pulled the two empty shells from their chambers, then dug in his pocket for some more, spilling the cartridges in his haste. Some fell in his lap, others hit the floor to roll away in the darkness sounding like thunder and lightning as they crossed the rough, wooden planks. But he pushed two home. He slid two shells into the shotgun and snapped it closed.

He lay still and silent again on the hard cot, listening as the shack creaked and groaned around him. Maybe it was Tom outside, maybe he'd only been unconscious, not really dead. But he knew it was impossible. In the darkness the memory of the torn man was excruciatingly vivid. And that was when he thought of the cat.

He tried to ignore the thought. He told himself it could be Cos outside. He remembered thinking he'd seen the old collie earlier. He was sure he'd seen something. And when he thought back on the memory, he was positive it hadn't been a shadow. He had thought it was Cos because of its shape, because of the way it had moved between the rocks. But now he realised it could just as easily have been the cat.

He could hardly see his hand in front of his face. He held the shotgun tight to his chest and fingered the twin triggers. He could feel the old fishermen's shack moving, swaying with the wind, could hear its ancient wooden walls and roof complaining. He swung his legs slowly, slowly off the cot and cautiously made his way towards where he thought the window was. He followed the sound of the driving rain crackling rapidly against the glass.

A gap in the clouds, and the pallid moon illuminated The Leap weakly. Joseph rubbed the cuff of his jumper on the smeared window. The fat drops of rain chasing each other down the outside of the glass distorted what he could see. He could make out the shapes of rocks, the movement of the river. Then the moon was gone again. He waited. He turned his head from the window so his breath wouldn't mist on the glass. He was shivering with the cold.

The door shook viciously in the wind. With an audible crack the bolt tore free of the rotten wood and the door slammed open, smashed itself closed and slammed open again. Joseph ran to it, fighting the wind for a grip on it, the icy rain in his face. He had to leave it to crash and flap while he dragged one of the cots over to hold it closed. And as he finally managed to stand the cot in place he saw it. The moon broke free of the cloud, The Leap, for a second or two, was washed in its dim luminescence, and from out of the corner of his eye Joseph saw it. Too pale to be a shadow, the cat moved along the edge of the river.

He grabbed the gun and ran to the window, but couldn't see beyond the night and the rain. It was out there, he'd seen it, he was sure he'd seen it. The storm lashed the outside of the shack. He couldn't hear beyond the creaking, rattling wood. He walked the inside walls, peering out of the gaps he'd tried to block with cots. Every movement he saw was the cat. Every noise he heard was the cat. It lurked in every shadow. It came a step closer every time his back was turned. He held the shotgun tight.

The roof groaned under the weight of . . . what? The wind? The cat? He staggered backwards into the middle of the room, banging painfully into the table in the dark, the shotgun pointed up into the air. He saw glimpses of sky through cracks in the timbers, shadows passing over them; maybe clouds . . .

The inside of the shack lit up like a camera flash, a Polaroid snapshot of the walls and cots. The roar of the shotgun came next. And Joseph was knocked on his backside, unable to see after the blinding flash, the negative of the shack branded on to his eyes. He was deaf with ringing ears. The gun hummed in his stinging hands, feeling hot. He'd put a hole in the roof the size of a football and the rain fell in.

He was sweating and breathing hard now. He fumbled with the gun until he was able to open it again, this time remembering how he'd done it. He didn't know which shell he'd fired, his fingers too numb to tell properly, so he discarded them both and put new ones in their place.

He was shaking. He waited by the window, his only real chance of seeing it, waiting for the cloud to clear. He *had* seen it, he told himself, he was sure he'd seen it. The gun was heavy, it became slick in the grip of his sweating palms. His fingers were forever playing against the triggers. He was so tired, but wouldn't let himself sleep. He scraped the barrels of the shotgun against the glass of the window. It sounded like fingernails on a blackboard. He didn't know what time it was, he had no idea how long he had to wait until daybreak. But he held the shotgun to him and refused to even lie down.

And when first light eventually came and he could see that the time on his watch said five thirty-eight, he was still standing by the window, still clutching the shotgun.

Chapter Nineteen

His mother was expecting them home today.

Joseph couldn't wake Don, but he could still hear his shallow breathing. He tore another strip of T-shirt to make a new bandage and had to peel the old one carefully away from the wound before he could tie it. And all the time he wasn't able to get that one thought out of his head: his mother was expecting them home today. He watched his father, he could almost see him fading away. And if he didn't make it, if he did die, then wouldn't that be what Joseph wanted? Wouldn't it be better for him at home without his father there?

He refused to think about it. His mother was expecting them home today, he told himself.

He stood by the window, watching, the gun in his hands. The rain had let up a little after daybreak but the wind was still as strong, it buffeted the tired little shack. He was watching for the cat. He knew it was out there somewhere and felt as if it was in turn watching for him. He also tried to scan the wall of the valley, knowing there must be a well-used path somewhere that would lead to the old road Tom and his father had talked about. Tom had said it was no longer there, but Joseph thought that if he could at least follow where it had once been then he'd be able to make it through the hills back to Becksall, to safety and help.

He was scared and tired. He didn't feel much like the adult he claimed to be any more, his true age of fifteen seemed all too real, all too small and fragile. He remembered thinking that he held some sort of power over the outcome of the weekend, and wondered just how much power he held now. He gripped the shotgun tighter still. But it didn't make him feel any more grown-up.

He watched for the cat for almost an hour before he dared to make a move. If he had waited any longer he didn't think he would have had the courage to move at all, but would have stayed inside the shack with his dying father, trapped by his own cowardice. He wished again that Cos was with him. Even if the dog couldn't lead him home it would at least have been company against the hills, and maybe an ally against the cat.

He checked his watch. It was just after seven. He checked on his father one last time, listened for his breathing, then pulled one of the cots to one side and squeezed himself out of the shack through a gap where a slat was missing. He struggled to pull the cot back into place again – he didn't think it would stop the cat from getting in at his father if it really wanted to, but it was the best he could do. He ran quickly towards the high, craggy wall of the valley, searching all the time for the path he hoped would lead up its side. He'd left his rucksack in the shack thinking it best not to be restricted by its bulk, as well as some food and a carton of Ribena for Don in case he came round. The rest of the food and the other three cartons of drink were stuffed inside his pockets. Only now as he ran did he realise he'd forgotten to pick up the shotgun cartridges he'd dropped last night.

Joseph hesitated. He didn't know whether to go back for them or not. He crouched down behind a boulder and counted the ones he still had with him. Six. He had six. Two in the gun and four in his pocket. He looked back at the shack standing next to the swollen river. But turned away. He was frightened that if he went back inside to retrieve the shells he'd probably lose his nerve and never pluck up the courage to make this run again.

He moved along the base of the valley wall, dodging between the rocks and boulders, searching for the way up the side the fishermen would have used. It had to be around here somewhere. If it existed. He tried to suppress the feeling he was being watched. He told himself it was only his imagination. Then he found it: a winding pathway leading up a shallow curve of the wall. It was still a steep climb, but the natural steps of rock along the way had been worn down even further by many years of big fishermen's boots and waders. He climbed carefully but quickly, checking over his shoulder at the shack and the valley below him. He felt a little too open as he climbed, a little too *on view*. The wind teased him; forever threatening to pull him off the narrow pathway, but never quite having the strength to do it. He left the shack a long way below and was glad to leave the close claustrophobia of the valley behind.

But his heart sank when he saw the hills. Bleak and cheerless they rolled away for ever and ever in every direction he turned. The wind whipped around him. Stronger now he was out of the valley, it stabbed at him through his clothes. He could see His Teeth in the distance, biting at the grey sky, and beyond them the sharp peak of Abraham's Height. Knowing their names gave him little comfort.

Again he thought about turning back. His mother was expecting them home today, and when they were only a minute late she'd be on the phone to the police, fire brigade, and hospitals. She'd have search parties out after them if only because he was meant to be back at school tomorrow.

He looked down into The Leap again. He was high above the shack and the river. How long did search parties usually take to find people? He suddenly wished he'd watched the 999 programme on TV more often.

He turned back to the hills. And it was seeing the remains of what must have been the old road which made up his mind. He still believed that if he followed it he would soon come to Becksall. That it would, that it must, eventually lead him back to the village.

It didn't look as though it had ever been a proper

road, there was no sign of tarmac, but it probably had been a track worn down by the weight of cars. It was grown over now with the coarse grass and heather which covered the rest of the hills, but the two parallel furrows in the ground were still quite clear as they ran away into the distance. All he had to do was walk inside one of the fat grooves and he'd be keeping to the road. He tried to follow the lines of the track into the distance with his eyes. But the hills seemed all too eager to hide their route. But if he kept to the ruts he'd be all right.

Joseph nodded to himself. The physical gesture helped him to believe in what he was telling himself. Then he started walking.

Joseph held his head down as he walked, partly to hide it from the wind, but also to watch he didn't step out of the track he was following. Occasionally he'd lift his eyes to look at the hills, but he had no way of gauging the distance he'd walked. His legs were already tired, the previous days' walking still heavy inside them. He followed the track as it rose and fell with the hills, as it took wide turns to avoid the steepest slopes and seemed to loop back on itself forever. He soon realised it was taking the long way down through the hills, taking the easiest route for vehicles, and his tired legs only seemed to fuel his frustration. Surely if he walked in a straight line it would be so much quicker? But he wouldn't leave the track. He didn't dare leave the track.

He tried to estimate how close to Becksall he was by how low in the hills he seemed to be. He knew the village was at the foot of the hills, and so thought that if the road led all the way there then it must surely come out of the hills pretty low down. But the road seemed to rise and fall with each and every hill it crossed, and at one time Joseph felt as if he'd been walking constantly up hill for well over half an hour. He became worried he'd strayed off the track, but he was still walking along the two furrows. And then he became frightened that this was another track, maybe one used by tractors, and he'd crossed on to it when he hadn't been concentrating.

He checked his watch more and more frequently. He began to think the minute hand was slow, maybe broken. But he told himself not to be stupid. He'd set himself a time of ten o'clock before he'd let himself eat and the hour took a day to drag itself around. At last, when it eventually came he sat himself down, to rest his legs while he ate. But the wind was too cold around him and so he ate as he walked, hoping to keep some of the warmth within his body. He checked his watch again after he'd finished the lump of pork-pie and it still read ten o'clock. He almost cried out in disbelief. It *had* been broken. It had slowed down until it had stopped altogether. He could quite literally have been walking for hours longer than his watch said he had.

The hills crowded around him, they weren't giving away any secrets. He couldn't tell the distance bet-ween them, how far he'd walked, how high he was up into them. Over every rise was another hill to climb, another mile to walk. They blocked out the rest of the world, they had him trapped inside them. The wind howled around him, screaming in the gullies, snatching at his clothes. His face stung with the cold, his cheeks felt raw. The hills rolled on and on. He was sure he was walking in circles, that the track he was following was in league with the hills. His legs ached with weariness. He had the collar of his coat turned up and his chin buried beneath the zip. His hands were shoved deep down in his pockets and the shotgun was clamped to his side with his arm.

He tried to concentrate on his feet, on where he was walking, on keeping within the two furrows. But in some places they weren't as clear as in others; in some places the grass seemed to have grown back over them a lot quicker, a lot thicker. And he felt as if the hills were hypnotising him. Their simple monotony, the way they confused distance and scale because he had nothing to compare them to except each other. He longed to see a telegraph pole, a tractor, a barn. Something man-made, something he knew the size of from memory that could put a perspective on the hills. He'd seen only two trees as he'd walked, both deformed and twisted, either broken and bent by the harsh wind or poisoned by the soil in which they grew.

He realised he hadn't thought of the cat in a long time, not since he'd set off from The Leap, and hackles of paranoia rose within him. He even pointed the gun and stood looking for it stalking through the grass after him. But paranoia was all it was, he told himself. He hadn't thought of the cat because he hadn't seen it, hadn't felt it. He put the gun back under his arm convinced he'd left it back at The Leap. But then he worried about his father being defenceless in the old shack.

He walked on. The track of the old road led him into rain. It was light at first, almost a mist, but the drops got heavier as the grey sky overhead opened up. Then the track forsook him altogether. He had no idea how far he'd walked, hunched against the rain, when he realised he was no longer following the twin furrows.

He bit back the sudden anxiety. It had claws in his heart as sharp as any cat's, but he held them at bay, he kept his head. He turned around and tried to retrace his steps exactly back the way he'd been walking for the last ten minutes or so. But he didn't come across the old road. He didn't know whether to carry on retracing his steps, and try further back still or not. He found furrows in the grass, ruts and grooves and indentations, some of them in pairs, they were all around when he looked for them. But nothing that looked like the road he'd been following only a short while before. If indeed it *was* the road he'd been following.

The hills seemed to lean in closer. Their peaks seemed to rise that little bit higher, crowding out even more of the sky, even more of what Joseph could only think of as the real world.

Still fighting the sharpness of the growing anxiety, still not willing to give in and run, he remembered Abraham's Height. If he could find the Height, he told himself, then he could find His Teeth. And maybe from there he could find his way back to Art Hooper's cottage. But through the sheets of rain he couldn't even make out the sides of the nearest hills, never mind any peaks that were sure to be several miles away.

He put his head down. He screwed his eyes tight shut. His bit his lip until blood came. But he still couldn't hold the panic slowly rising in him. It was hot; it would burn his eyes and steam his mind.

He walked. He walked to dull the sensation. He sang to himself. He kept forgetting the words to his favourite songs, so made them up instead. He sang his made-up words out loud. He shouted them into the icy wind and pelting rain. He remembered his Walkman, he remembered he'd left it in his rucksack. He didn't care about losing the road now, he just wanted to find a way down. Any way down. He pushed through some straggly bushes, scratching his hands. And then he remembered Gavin Fisher from the juniors.

Joseph had sat at the desk next to Gavin in the second year. Gav had rusty-red hair, loads of freckles and a stutter which got worse whenever teachers asked him to read aloud – and they had eventually stopped asking him altogether. But Joseph had liked him, mainly because he'd always let Joseph copy his answers during the spelling tests Miss Granger had given the class every week. And one day Gav had come into school carrying a Roses chocolate box, and everyone had crowded around the desk to see if they could scrounge one off him. But he hadn't had any chocolates in this box, oh no. He'd said his cat had given him a present. He'd said his cat often gave him presents, left them for him on the doorstep, and he'd brought this one in to school to show Miss Granger. He'd said his cat was called Sooty. He'd tipped up the old Roses chocolate box and a dead blue tit had tumbled out on to the clean pages of Joseph's new maths book. Its wings had been open as if in full flap, and its head had been bitten clean off. All the girls had screamed while all the boys had said it looked really cool.

Joseph remembered Gavin Fisher when he found Cos's body at the bottom of the escarpment.

Chapter Twenty

The cat was all around him now.

He spun around, turning this way and that, peering through the rain, the shotgun in front of him. It was following him. It was out there. A noise behind him . . .

The gun boomed, thumping him backwards and he slipped on the grass, falling again. But he got to his feet, trying to make out shapes in the sheets of rain.

It pelted down on the old collie's dead body, soaking the dark fur, pooling with the bright blood. He walked backwards away from it, feeling the cat all around him, spinning and turning with the gun. The rain hid so many shapes. It stung his eyes, ran in icy rivers down his neck. His hair was plastered flat to his head and he pushed his fringe higher up out of his eyes. His hands were numb on the cold metal of the gun. He kept walking away, kept checking over his shoulder, turning with the gun. The grass and mud were slick beneath his feet.

He blew the rain from out of his mouth. He tried to wipe it away from his eyes with the sleeve of his coat. He couldn't see properly. His eyes were playing tricks on him. The rain was playing tricks on him. The hills were playing tricks on him. He didn't see the ground dip away. He missed his footing, slipping on the grass, and tumbled down the steep escarpment. He slipped and skidded on his back, rolling over through the mud, sliding down. He clutched the gun to him as he fell, not willing to give it up.

He scrambled to gain his feet. He'd twisted his ankle, but he could still stand. The pain was hot in his leg, but he could still walk. His hands were trembling, he told himself it was with the cold.

Shadows in the rain, running past him from out of the corner of his eye, and again the shotgun boomed. Its roar punched into his shoulder, knocking him backwards. But he kept his feet.

The hills rising above him, the cloud pressing him down. The cat was out there. It had killed Tom, it had killed Cos. It was following him. It was hunting him.

He turned and ran.

He ran blindly, foolishly, through the driving rain.

Slipping and skidding down the slopes of th.., his ankle burning. All he could think about was Tom. All he could see in his mind's eye was Tom Beverly lying face-down in the dirt. He ran through a flock of sheep crowding together against the weather, scattering them higher up the hillside. Maybe the cat would go after them. Their bleating, mewling complaints chased him on the wind.

He couldn't see the cat behind him, only shifting, fleeting images through the rain. But he knew it was there. He could almost hear it at his shoulder: the hissing, spitting cry of a demon.

His breath was ragged, his heart hammered at his chest. There was a solid chunk of fear in his throat and he was unable to swallow. The gun was so heavy in his hand, but he wouldn't let it go. He slithered down another embankment, gouging great tracks in the mud to keep his balance. The rain lashed down on his face, stinging his eyes. It wanted to fill his mouth and choke him every time he tried to draw a breath.

It was only a story, he told himself. He was a preacher now. It was just a legend. The cat was the devil chasing him across the hills.

'It's only a story,' he shouted. 'It's only a story.'

But the hills didn't seem to be listening.

His ankle throbbed, it wanted to buckle beneath him. Tom's bald head had been clawed and bloody, and Cos was dead. He saw the cat leap and screamed out, falling to his knees. But couldn't tell whether it had just been the memory in his head, or the shadows in the rain.

He couldn't stand again, his ankle wouldn't let him. He could feel the pain pulsing up through his leg. 'You've got the most to lose,' Art Hooper told him. Tom Beverly fell to his knees with a pale ghost on his back.

Joseph crawled through the tangled gorse and hid himself between the rocks. He fought to reload the shotgun, and won. Snapping it shut, breathing hard. The hurt in his ankle was sickening; dizziness rolled like waves through his head. Movement behind him . . . Both barrels roared at once. And the sheep was flipped over and torn open before his eyes. Its body slid on the slick grass and red, red blood trickled down the short slope towards him.

Chapter Twenty-one

He only realised he'd fainted when he opened his eyes again.

They fluttered open slowly, giving him snapshots of the gorse bush, the rocks, the muddy slope of the hill. His ankle had bloated, ballooned to twice its size and was pushing painfully against the sides of his boot. He could smell the sickly, sweet stench of the dead sheep. He had its blood on his hands. He kicked the body away from him with his good leg.

It had stopped raining, although the dark clouds still seemed very low over the hills. Carefully he raised himself up so he could lean back against the rocks. He was shivering in his wet clothes. He looked out over the bushes, scanning the hillside for movement, turning around to look up behind him. But could see nothing.

He went to reload the gun. He broke it open and dug in his pockets for the last two cartridges. He tried another pocket. He tried his jeans. He was sure he'd had two more. He searched the ground around him. He *had* to have two more. But they'd been lost. He dug in his pockets again but only found an empty drink carton which had burst open when he'd fallen, and the crushed, soggy remains of the pork-pie.

He felt the panic in him again. Like a mushroom cloud it burst in his belly and rose up through the rest of his body.

But he held it down, he forced it back. He closed his eyes against it and wouldn't let it come. He took deeper breaths, holding each one for the count of ten. And gradually the feeling cooled as it slipped away. He talked to himself, calming himself. And although the shotgun was useless to him now he held on to it as tightly as ever. He wouldn't let it go.

Once again he looked out over the hillside. The hills fell away from here; he seemed to be at one of the highest points and could see a ragged pattern of fields in the distance. Maybe Becksall is down there too, he told himself.

Walking was slow and painful; he hobbled awkwardly on his twisted ankle, often slipping and falling. His wet clothes were heavy, they felt as though they were dragging him down. But the sensation that he was getting closer was too strong to give up. It was mostly downhill now. He chose the steeper slopes and slid down them on his backside, the grass still greasy from the rain.

He watched for the cat always. He was constantly checking over his shoulder, ducking down behind rocks to rest and wait in case it was following him. But he never saw it. And the fact began to play on his mind.

He knew that since escaping The Leap he hadn't actually seen the cat, and even then he couldn't truly be sure he'd seen it near the old fishermen's shack anyway. He began to wonder if it had all been his imagination. It could have killed Cos at any time, he reasoned. The old dog could have tried to return home during the night and the cat could have attacked it then. And why would the cat be following me anyway? he thought. Surely it would eat Tom before looking for more food (but he pushed this thought away; he pushed it deep down in his head).

He knew all this sounded reasonable, he spoke it aloud to himself as he walked and it all sounded true and sensible. But he still checked over his shoulder and he still crouched behind rocks.

Night was coming on. The hills were darkening quickly, helped on by the thick clouds that clogged up the sky. He began to worry now, he didn't want to be trapped in the hills for another night. He was exhausted and cold and knew how much colder it would get before morning. Every time he came to a crest in the hills he tried to gauge how far away the ragged pattern of fields was now, but they didn't seem to be getting any closer. He began to feel as though he was chasing the end of the rainbow. But he bit back against the pain in his ankle and walked on.

He began telling himself the things he'd do when he got home.

'When I get home,' he said, 'when I get home I'm going to rearrange all my covers on my wall. When I get home I'm going to take my mum to the pictures. When I get home I'm going to tell Sarah Beechwood that I love her. When I get home I'm going to . . .'

But he couldn't think of one for his father.

It was dark now, he'd lost sight of the fields and could

only hope he was walking in the right direction. The night was cold and heavy around him and he couldn't keep thoughts of the cat at bay. There were noises in the night that he hadn't heard during the day. His ankle had swollen even bigger and he stumbled along on it, biting his lip every time his weight pressed down. He'd had to undo the laces of his boot.

He scooted on his backside down a little slope. He was fighting against the fear brought on by the horrible realisation that he might have to spend another night in the hills. He stood up, hobbling forward, and suddenly he wasn't walking on grass or mud any more. The mixture of feelings running through him was almost too strong, almost too overpowering. He was walking on a road, he'd found a road. He stamped his good foot on the tarmac. He'd found a road. And a road had to lead him somewhere. No matter how long it took, eventually it had to go *somewhere.*

Chapter Twenty-two

His ankle still burned. The wind tugged at his clothes and the dampness of the night clung to him. But he was getting somewhere, he was sure of that. Just as long as he didn't lose the road like he had the old track. And he wasn't quite able to shake that little, pricking feeling of paranoia, so he stopped every few minutes and either crouched to touch the hard road surface with his fingers or stamped on it with his good foot.

He stopped every time he heard noises in the night. He listened against the wind as it whipped around him, and strained to see into the darkness, hiding behind the useless shotgun. Because he knew the cat was still out there. But the wind stuffed his ears like cotton wool, like cotton wool full of static, and he found it so hard to make sense of the noises it carried. He had to rely on his eyes. And they could see no further than the twin barrels of the shotgun.

He stopped because he needed to rest. He was

tired, exhausted. He stood on one foot, his good foot, holding his throbbing ankle in the air to try and ease it a little. He knew he wouldn't be able to walk much further. He couldn't walk much further. He sweated even though his body was terribly cold. But he had to go on, because if he didn't . . . His exhaustion was like a lead weight across his shoulders, breaking his back.

He stopped and tried to gauge the road. He ran his hand along its surface. He walked on a little further and was sure he could feel it sloping away beneath him. But the harder he concentrated, the more confused he became. One moment he'd be confident it was leading him down out of the hills, then the next he'd stumble as he misjudged his footing and be certain it was rising to take him higher into them. It twisted and snaked beneath him, seeming almost desperate to throw him off its back. It took him blind round sharp bends where the cat could so easily have been waiting, it cut back against itself, it narrowed and widened at will. So he stopped every few minutes and either crouched to touch the hard road surface with his fingers or stamped on it with his good foot.

*

The moon was very low in the sky, barely above the hills, though it was brighter than he had ever seen it before. He followed it, he walked towards it and held on to it with his eyes. But his eyes were playing tricks on him again because he felt as though he was getting closer to it with every step.

The thought frightened him. He tried to gauge the road again, worried in case he was climbing higher and higher into the hills without realising it. His eyes were watering with the stinging wind and he tried his best to clear them, blinking the pain away.

He was going crazy; there was no way he could walk to the moon. He physically shook his head in a vain attempt to untangle his thoughts. But it was getting closer, it really was. He was catching the moon. He stared up above his head, trying to find some stars behind the clouds – was he getting closer to them too? And that was when he saw a second moon, much dimmer than the first. And that was when he realised he was following the light from a distant window.

It was all he could do to stop himself from running. The pain in his ankle was suddenly no longer sharp enough to stop him. Every hobbled step was bringing him closer. He could almost make out the shape of the building ahead of him. His eyes still blurred the light, but it was now so obviously a window. He had to force himself to keep to the road; he wanted to cut the winding corners but knew losing the road would be a terrible mistake. Yet it was still a fight not to try.

It was so easy to ignore the pain and the cold and the exhaustion now. He could hear voices in the night, pulling him towards the light, and The Retreat stood among the hills not more than a hundred metres in front of him. He started shouting. 'Hey! Hey, Lizzie! Help! Please help me!' And he was running as fast as he could with his feeble ankle. 'Help me! Help me, Lizzie!' The wind savagely stuffed his voice back down his throat, but he still shouted. The hills clung on to him, didn't want to let him go, but he tore at the thick, blustery night with his numb fingers and got closer and nearer with every stumbling step.

And the voices got louder, the light brighter. The Retreat closer. It grew out of the night to become solid and real in front of him. He thought he saw people pass the window, their silhouettes flickering by the light, and shouted to them. He thought he could pick out Lizzie's voice from the rest of the noise.

There was a small car and a battered transit van

parked in the small lay-by. He ran towards them.
And the cat stepped out into the road from behind
them.

Chapter Twenty-three

'No,' Joseph said. He was shaking his head. 'No.'

He held the shotgun out in front of him, he aimed it uselessly, stupidly, at the cat. Its lips peeled back from its teeth as it hissed at him. It stood between him and The Retreat. Between him and the lights and the voices. He stood behind the gun like a child hiding from his nightmares behind his pillow.

The cat stepped towards him. It was so pale in the night; its eyes were pricks of sharp light. Its long tail swept slowly back and forth as it took another step. He saw its shoulders rise like slow pistons high on its back. Its snarl was low, spiteful.

For Joseph there was no way out. The Retreat was so close but still too far to run to. He shouted against the wind. His ankle throbbed, he could hardly stand on it. He waved the gun weakly. He saw Tom in the dirt, he saw Cos in the mud. The cat moved so slowly towards him, its eyes on his every move. Its tail swept hypnotically back and forth, its teeth were vicious through its low snarls. It was closing the space between them, its paws coming down gently, softly on the road, so sure of its prey.

He was so close. But he was going to die. Shudders ran through him, shaking him. 'No,' he said. 'No.' The light was so close.

The cat was going to kill him. He was going to die. He stood behind the worthless shotgun. He knew it was worthless but simply wasn't able to take his hands from it. He was stepping backwards. He was going to die. He started to cry.

'Please. Please, no.'

He was looking to his left, to his right. He couldn't see a way out. The cat was baring its teeth as it came, daring him to run. It would bring him down in a second. It would leap at his back and rip him open with its teeth. It wanted him to run.

He could have touched it. He could have reached out and patted its head. Its eyes were fixed on his. One more step and it would kill him. A slash of its claws. A snap of its teeth. One more step. And he could do nothing about it except shake his head and cry. He was as worthless and as impotent as the shotgun he held.

The cat didn't take its eyes from him. But it didn't come any closer. It hissed at him, it spat its hatred at him. It bared its teeth one last time. Then simply walked away.

It turned its back on him, confident that he couldn't hurt it. It dropped its gaze and turned away as if it knew how weak he really was. It could have pitied him. He felt as if it knew how little he could do to defend himself. He couldn't harm it. He could do nothing to hurt it. It walked away from something too small to concern it. And it slipped back into the night as easily as it had appeared, the darkness of the hills eager to hide it from view.

Chapter Twenty-four

The moon was hidden behind the clouds as they moved across the night sky. The wind whistled and howled around the roof and eaves of the small country pub. The yellow light from the window fell into the little lay-by that served as a carpark and on to the van and the car that stood there. Alone on the tarmac, the boy's legs had finally given up. He sobbed silently into his hands, the shotgun discarded on the ground next to him. His slight shoulders shook. His eyes were squeezed tight shut, but the tears still ran in rivulets through the dirt on his face.

Without even touching him the cat had torn him in two. It had hurt him, broken him, scarred him and not left a mark. His skin was still clean. He had said he wanted the cat to kill his father, but he knew it had done much worse to him. He would never again be able to walk alone at night. He would never feel safe again when he wasn't looking behind, when he wasn't checking over his shoulder. He would forever feel hunted, forever be prey.

And he knew of only two others who would ever be able to understand this. But Tom Beverly was dead.

He looked up at The Retreat. He could hear the voices from inside, numbed by the wind that tugged at his clothes and hair. He hoped someone would find him soon. He hoped someone would come outside and see him in the road because he didn't think he could walk any more. He didn't have the strength to move any more. He needed someone to help him get out of the cold. His tears were as icy as the night around him.

And he hoped it was someone who would listen to him, he had so much to say. He wanted to tell them all about Sarah Beechwood, he wanted to tell them about his covers. He wanted to tell them about his father. Because if they were quick enough, they might be able to save his life.

Robert Leeson

Doomwater

She turned to look downstream into the depths of the millpool and her heart turned to ice inside her. There was a drumming in her ears, her lungs strained for breath, as if the dark waters were rising from their bed and closing over her.

Charlotte, orphaned as a child, has grown into a happy and fun-loving teenager. But there is a darker side to her nature, perfectly illustrated by her painting, 'Doomwater', which shows someone drowning in a pool.

But why does Charlotte have such a fascination with water and drowning? And will her fascination turn into a self-fulfilling prophecy?

Frances Usher

Face to Face

Someone was laughing and calling me. I didn't hear the words, just the voice, but I knew I was the one being called. Someone was calling and teasing and laughing. Where? Behind me? . . . No, in front. Or was it only in my head?

Nick's dreams are driving him mad – running down endless corridors where he is haunted by the laughter of a girl with dark hair. Are the dreams a warning that destiny will bring him together with the unknown girl in a terrible way? And then Nick sees the girl on a school bus . . .

Sue Welford

Dreamstalker

Behind her, the footfalls began again. Each one of her strides was matched by someone else. She began to jog, then run, gasping for breath. The person behind began to run too, the footfalls getting closer, closer . . . catching up.

When Nikki visits her penfriend in the country, strange things start to happen. There are noises in the attic and Nikki begins to have frightening dreams. She's convinced the house is haunted and that the ghost is trying to tell her something. But why her? And who is it that is just one step behind her wherever she goes?